IT'S ALL ABOUT THE HEART

A NOVEL

To Colleen
Happy Reading!
Lenore Schur

LENORE SCHUR

True Potential
REACH THE WORLD

Unless otherwise noted, Scripture is taken from the New King James Version®. Copyright © 1982 by Thomas Nelson. Used by permission. All rights reserved.

It's All About the Heart

Cover and Interior Page design by True Potential, Inc.

ISBN: 978-1-943852-39-0 (paperback)
ISBN: 978-1-943852-40-6 (ebook)

Library of Congress Control Number: 2016961504

True Potential, Inc
PO Box 904, Travelers Rest, SC 29690
www.truepotentialmedia.com
Printed in the United States of America.

*To my Mom who believed that one day
I would be exceptional.*

CONTENTS

Chapter 1 7

Chapter 2 17

Chapter 3 24

Chapter 4 33

Chapter 5 41

Chapter 6 56

Chapter 7 61

Chapter 8 72

Chapter 9 85

Chapter 10 99

About the Author 109

Resources 111

CHAPTER 1

THE WIND SWIRLED THROUGH THE TREES WHILE A gust of cold air slapped Jannie in the face as she walked toward the line of buildings at the end of the street. Ten more steps. She lifted the collar on her coat and clasped it with her left hand to keep the icy draft from blowing on her neck. Just as she reached the entrance of the first grey stone building, a splash of rain hit her.

"No umbrella," she thought. She pushed the heavy wooden door open and stumbled inside. The warm smell of coffee and baked goods enveloped her, helping her to quickly forget where she had just been. Jannie's eyes surveyed the room. She selected a small round table next to the fireplace and slung her coat over the chair. As she dug through her handbag to find her wallet, a figure crossed between her and the light of the window casting a shadow on the table. She looked up to see a familiar smiling face.

"Well, hello, Derek, what brings you here?"

"Probably the same thing as you—a hot cup of coffee to break up a cold blustery afternoon."

"Well, that is my excuse. Sit down and I'll grab some for you."

"No, I'll get it. I want to celebrate the end of the semester anyway. So it is my treat, today."

"Okay," said Jannie, dropping into the chair. "Cream and sugar, please."

Jannie sifted through papers in her schoolbag before selecting a stack of papers with handwritten notes.

Derek had walked by that house many weeks before he realized someone from his school lived there.

"Whatcha got there?" asked Derek as he slid Jannie's coffee across the table and seated himself across from her.

"These are the forms to confirm my classes for next semester. For some reason I just can't seem to get them filled out."

"Procrastination got the best of you?"

"Well, it's more like hesitation. I don't have the same enthusiasm for this course that I had when I started it a year and a half ago. I'm not even able to pinpoint why."

"Hmm, this seems to be a line of study you've been looking forward to for a long time, right?" Derek and Jannie had known each other since they were in junior high school. Derek's parents had moved to the city after his dad's job had ended abruptly at the refinery. They moved into the neighborhood where Jannie had been living all her life. In fact, her family lived in the same rambling old house that her father had grown up in. Derek had walked by that house many weeks before he realized someone from his school lived there. Jannie, who was a year younger, had been on her way to school one morning when Derek spotted her. He ran to catch up with her, and they soon began walking to school together everyday. When Derek went off to college a year before her, Jannie found it difficult not to be able to converse with him everyday. But days turned into weeks and soon life took another turn, and they each had their own separate lives. Now they sat across from each other, drinking hot coffee as the wind outside heralded a coming storm.

"You know you don't have to continue, don't you?" Derek looked intently at Jannie, his eyes locking her in a mesmerizing gaze.

"What exactly are you saying?"

"Well, I know you were determined to get your degree, but if you are almost half way through and questioning your next move, that may be an indication of something deeper going on."

"Like what?"

"That it is not what you are called to do."

"Called?" Jannie questioned.

"The older I get, the more I believe we need to find our calling in life and not just settle for what others may think we should do. Often our career choices are based on remuneration…"

"That's a pretty big word," she interrupted, chuckling and playfully trying to steer him off course.

Derek was not that easily distracted. "You've got to admit that most of the people we finished high school with, decided their vocation after checking the salaries they would be making. Although that's well and good, we all need money to survive. I really think we should not base our life's work solely on how much money we are going to make."

"Yes, I hear you, but that's at the forefront of everyone's mind. I think we are not going to change society's view of it any time soon."

"No, but we don't have to conform to it in our lives." Derek raised his eyebrows and tilted his head as if to punctuate his statement and get Jannie's affirmation.

"So," Jannie queried, "How exactly do I know what my calling in life is? Surely it lies in what I am good at and what I am interested in. Am I right?"

"Sure, I don't believe you are going to be called to be a nurse if you faint at the very sight of blood. But we may have talents that are for our own pleasure and not to be turned into a life-long career, even though they are something we are really good at."

"Hmmm, you make a good point." Jannie looked down at the stack of papers she had in front of her. "I suppose this is something I should consider now instead of finishing my degree and then finding out I took a wrong turn."

"You know the expression about someone missing their calling? For example, the guy working in a machine shop by day, getting all greasy and dirty, and he has the most incredible sense of humor. But the guys at the shop are the only ones who benefit from it. Here he is, cracking jokes, making the guys laugh uncontrollably, but he has an audience of two or three. Then his co-workers start telling their friends, 'Man, my co-worker Joe really missed his calling. He should be doing stand up comedy in clubs or have a show on a national network. But here he is doing grunt work with us and nobody knows how funny a comedian he is. What a waste of talent'. That's what I mean, Jannie. There are gifts and callings in us, and I believe it is up to us to figure them out sooner than later."

"That's very deep, Derek, but it doesn't help me one bit!" Jannie laughed and took another sip of the hot coffee. As she let it trickle down her throat, she realized how much she had missed her daily talks with Derek. This was refreshing.

"Maybe this will help you put things in perspective. I read a blog written by this lady who is a writer. She knew she was called all her life but struggled to convince others that it was a worthwhile profession. I'll find it and you can read it."

What exactly is a job and why do many people balk at the idea of getting one?.

Derek pulled out his computer tablet and began searching.

"Here it is. I will send it to you. Better yet, I will read it—it's not that long."

It's called **Just go get a job**.

Have you ever said that phrase to anyone? Has anyone said it to you? Regardless of who is delivering it, the phrase is often accompanied by a lot of emotion, usually negative. What exactly is a job and why do many people balk at the idea of getting one?

Here are a few definitions of 'job': the process or requirements of working; anything a person is expected or obliged to do; duty; responsibility; a post of employment; a specific task done as part of the routine of one's occupation or for an agreed price.

The societies of North America are thought to have been founded on a Protestant work ethic. The idea behind it emphasizes hard physical labour, discipline and frugal living, and it dates back to ancestral European cultures. Even though our culture has been redefined over the last 300 years, a stigma remains today, albeit subtle, that worships anyone who follows those guidelines. Your worth is determined by whether or not you have a job and especially whether or not you have a 'good job'. Herein lies the problem—judging people based on what they do for a living.

Remember the song "Get a Haircut and Get a Real Job"? George Thorogood wrote that song in response to his parents' distaste for his vocation. But during his 40-year career, he recorded more than 20 albums, and his current net worth is about $50 million. I guess he didn't need a real job. Dire Straits echoed a similar theme in "Money For Nothing." Obviously, the song's subject/narrator didn't consider performing music on TV a real job. In his mind, "that ain't workin'."

Many times our career path is picked because of safety—the safety of having money. Don't get me wrong; it is not the money that is the issue. However, when money is the only motivation, it can lead to a life of dissatisfaction.

Dr. Marsha Sinetar wrote a book, "Do What You Love, The Money Will Follow." In the introduction she wrote, "I began to experience a great longing to change my life. The thought of letting go of what I had—a well-paying, secure job—was truly terrifying. I who had always clung to outward forms of security... also ignored the inner dissatisfactions and urgings I felt."

Meg Ryan's character in the movie "You've Got Mail" is quoted as saying, "I lead a small life... do I do it because I like it or because I haven't been brave?" Jeff Goins says, "What most people call being 'lazy' is really just fear. Fear of failure. Fear of rejection. Fear, fear, fear."

My uncle worked as a bus driver for 30 years. Upon retirement, he got a gold watch. During the span of his career, he was considered a stable, reliable, 'good worker' by his colleagues. I wonder though, how he felt every day as he got up, donned his *uniform and clocked in on another shift. Did he enjoy himself because he was doing what he always wanted to do or did he settle into the job because he made a decent wage? Was it his calling or did he simply do it out of fear? I guess we won't know. He is in a nursing home now, sitting quietly in a wheelchair. No one can see his gold watch.*

No doubt, you've heard the phrase that a person missed his or her calling. It is often a reference to someone awing an audience with their talents when in real life, they work a routine job that they highly dislike. According to author and speaker Craig Hill, "a century ago, people prepared their children to fulfill their calling. Now parents educate children in hopes that they will get a good job or occupation." We are now working to get money instead of spending time fulfilling our calling.

We've lost our vision in the pursuit of provision.

What is the alternative? I hear the extremist stay, "Not work? We all need money to live." Yes, in our society, we do. But it was not always that way. My great-grandfather came here from Austria and began farming a piece of land. The government's offer of a homestead to immigrants was how he got established. I can't tell you for sure if he had any money. What I do know is that he had enough livestock and produce to support his family of eight and into the next generation. The point is the focus was not on amassing a large sum of money. He focused on building a family and a life in which that family could be sustained and subsequently thrive.

We are no longer living because we are too caught up in making a living.

As a result of focusing on money, we have actually destroyed human relationships. Our society has become so self absorbed that we don't even consider future generations.

Fortunately, not every individual conforms to this mentality. Meet Dale Partridge. Dale is a serial entrepreneur who teaches organisations about brand positioning. He tells the story of his dad coming home from work and saying, "Dale, I am wearing the golden handcuffs." What his dad meant was he had a job he considered too good to leave. But instead of being a disgruntled worker, he turned his attention to his son and groomed him for life as an entrepreneur. It worked. Dale made more than $25 million before he was 30.

I am not against getting a job. If you've got absolutely nothing, go sweep the parking lot at the local burger joint. We all have to start somewhere. What I am saying is, as soon as possible, stop trading hours for dollars and start living out your calling. I am frustrated with hearing from people who would just like to stuff everyone into a box labelled 'job'. When you stick your hand in the box, you pull out descriptions. They may read, 'Monday to Friday, 9 to 5', 'must have post secondary education' or 'minimum five-figure income'. The point is this does not allow for an entrepreneurial spirit, giftings or talents.

I am also not berating formal education. If you are called to be a teacher, get a degree and teach. But if your calling is to be a ditch digger, do it proudly and with all your heart. Just don't settle for a life inside the box. I, personally, can't count the times people have condescendingly told me to lose the pipe dream of being a writer and just go get a job. But I defiantly refuse. To quote Jeff Goins again, "for me, writing is a calling. It's not something I chose; it chose me. That's who I am."

Having said that, I know I am setting myself up for a lot of criticism. But, ahhh, I am up to it.

After all, it is my job.

Derek looked up from the tablet. His gaze was fixed on Jannie's face as if to punctuate his point.

"We all make the same mistake. We believe the lie that we are to go where the money is. But if we were to go where our heart says to go, the doors would open for us to fulfil our calling once we got there."

If you've got absolutely nothing, go sweep the parking lot at the local burger joint. We all have to start somewhere.

Jannie thought for a moment. What the writer of the blog said was so true. Why didn't schools teach things like this? What now?

"I have an idea," Derek broke into her thoughts. He reached into his back pocket and produced a tattered black wallet that seemed way too full for someone who was in school and didn't have a lot of money. As he opened it, it revealed many business cards, some as worn as the wallet. He fingered a few and pulled out a plain white card with black lettering in the middle. There were no other markings on the card. The three lines contained a name, address and phone number, in that order. He slid the card across the table and Jannie picked it up.

"I believe this might be of help."

Mr. Sherman
17 Gloster Lane
555-1212

"What's this?" asked Jannie, looking at Derek with inquisitive eyes. "I guess I should ask, who is this?"

"Well, Mr. Sherman is a long time friend of my dad, and his wife recently moved to a care facility, so he is alone most of the day—other than his helper who comes in to make him meals and clean the house. She's not really much company for him, though. It's more of a job to her, and she's not a great conversationalist."

"He really just needs a companion. Someone to sit and drink afternoon tea with and have a chat about things."

"But what has this got to do with me? How is this supposed to help me decide my future? Is this man some sort of—"

"He really just needs a companion. Someone to sit and drink afternoon tea with and have a chat about things. He doesn't get around very well, but his mind is razor sharp. I am sure it would be good for both of you."

Jannie gave Derek the most bewildered look she could fashion.

Derek glanced at his watch and quickly jumped up from the table.

"Sorry, got to go. I will call you in a couple of days."

"Thanks for the coffee," Jannie called after him, but he simply smiled and scurried out of the building.

Jannie fiddled with the card for a few moments before gathering her belongings and heading out the door. What was Derek up to? A companion to an old man? Hmmm, this might be an interesting diversion.

CHAPTER 2

JANNIE SLOWED DOWN AND SCANNED THE LONG row of cookie cutter houses until she spied the misfit.

"Yup, this must be it," she thought to herself. Mr. Sherman's house was at least 30 years older than the rest of the subdivision. It looked as if it had been dropped into the middle of the development by some giant crane. Once she parked and started her way up the walk, Jannie became absorbed in the myriad of plants that lined both sides of the concisely placed stones. These were not random placements but a carefully constructed garden and one that was meticulously cared for by a skilled hand.

Jannie was greeted by Ms. Brookes, a polite lady dressed in what she may have considered a business suit. Ms. Brookes looked like she belonged in an office with her hair tightly curled against her head and a coordinating scarf wound around her neck.

She didn't smile as she greeted Jannie.

"Mr. Sherman is waiting for you on the patio," she stated in a very professional manner. Ms. Brookes led the way through the house and onto a stone patio that overlooked the back yard. Mr.

Sherman was seated in a wicker chair with flowered cushions well worn from his afternoon rituals. He raised himself and extended his hand. The other hand remained on the arm of the chair to help him balance. He smiled warmly.

"Good afternoon, I trust you found the place quite easily."

"Oh, yes," Jannie replied. "I was given really good directions."

"Well, sit down and let's have a cup of tea together. Ms. Brookes will bring it out for us, won't you, dear?" Mr. Sherman looked towards Ms. Brookes, but she had already disappeared into the kitchen where a tray with tea and goodies had already been prepared. She returned almost instantly and began pouring tea into fancy teacups set on matching saucers. The spoons were a silverplate—highly polished and gleaming in the afternoon sun. Cloth napkins, perfectly pressed and folded, rounded out the tea service.

"My wife always insisted that afternoon tea be served only on fine china. I tend to agree. It makes me feel worthy of the ritual."

"My wife always insisted that afternoon tea be served only on fine china. I tend to agree. It makes me feel worthy of the ritual." Jannie smiled at how easily Mr. Sherman shared his thoughts. He was not at all stuffy like she imagined an 85-year-old could be. He talked freely about the past and the present with little change of emotion. He simply stated facts as facts in a "nothing you can do about them so why bother getting upset" sort of way.

"I understand you are wanting to put your degree on hold for a bit," said Mr. Sherman. "No harm in that. I always found that the best lessons were learned through experience and not from books. Not that I don't like books. I will show you my library. I am sure you will agree that it is extensive. It seems, though, that the lessons that stick with us are the ones we learn with our hearts."

Jannie studied Mr. Sherman as he spoke. His face was soft and his gaze looked off past the row of trees lining his property.

Jannie sat quietly, listening to Mr. Sherman relate many incidents that made up his life. From almost missing the ship that was to take him to his newly chosen country of residence to the chance meeting of his future wife in a hotel lobby. He spoke affectionately of his wife who had been his best friend, his confidante, his advisor and his love. Though she spent most of her days in a bed in a nearby nursing home, he never missed an opportunity to have breakfast with her. It had been their morning ritual for more decades than either of them could tell you. His fondness for her was evident in every word he spoke. "Isabella," he called her. He had never shortened it or replaced it with a cute nickname. That is who she was to him and it never changed. The afternoon sped by too quickly for Jannie, and she soon found herself saying good-bye. As Jannie announced it was time to leave, Mr. Sherman promised to resume his narrative when she returned.

"I will be back to see you on Thursday," she said as he walked her to the front door. His gait was quite steady with the help of a cane.

"Great. We will have tea in the library. That is my second favourite room in the house." He smiled with his eyes, proving much life was left in them.

A few days later, Jannie found herself again ascending the walk to Mr. Sherman's house. With each step, she felt herself become more relaxed as the plants absorbed the weight she was happy to shed. The shrubs stood confidently, vowing to protect against any inclement weather that blew in, and the efflorescence heralded her approach.

"Good afternoon, Jannie," the delight was evidenced in Mr. Sherman's voice. He had been waiting for her inside the front hallway that led to the back of the house. "As promised, we will have our tea in the library. This way."

Jannie followed as Mr. Sherman shuffled down the hallway with the aid of his cane. As they rounded the corner, she caught sight of a set of double doors that led to the library. They stretched almost to the ceiling and arched at the top like a cathedral entrance. The stout wooden doors spoke of centuries of knowledge contained behind them as they opened to reveal a room unlike the others in the house. Books of every imaginable genre lined the walls on three sides of the room. It was difficult to focus on one particular point because there was so much for the eye to absorb. Mr. Sherman picked out a worn leather chair near the one large window at the opposite end of the room. It, too, stretched from floor to ceiling, half rounded at the top as if to reflect the image of the entrance. Jannie sat next to him, peering out onto the manicured terrace as Ms. Brookes appeared with a tray of pastries.

"Tell me about your wife, Mr. Sherman. How is she doing?"

"Yes, Isabella." His face softened and his voice became mellow. "She is a dear. Her mind is perfectly clear and her memory impeccable. Unfortunately, her body is wearing out. The care aides get her out of bed and sit her in a chair each morning, but she is yet unable to walk on her own. She was fine living here until she broke her hip. It's sad but it's still delightful that I can see her every day. The nursing home is but a few blocks from here, so each day I get to have breakfast with her. I even make it back some evenings and sit with her before she goes to bed. We have had her back here on a few occasions. She absolutely loves it, and we talk about the possibility of her being able to walk again and return home. It might be several months yet, though."

His voice broke off, and Jannie could see he was deep in thought. She decided not to pry any further and just wait until he spoke of her again on his own. He seemed to take a deep interest in what Jannie was doing. It was probably a good distraction for him. It gave him opportunity to be around young people since his and Isabella's two sons were out of the country. In fact both lived across the ocean. Neither of them had married nor had they any family of their own.

"Have you made any progress on your career choice?" Mr. Sherman asked while pouring steaming brown liquid into a dainty cup.

"It's definitely consuming my thought life, but I can't say I have had made any decisions regarding it. I suppose I haven't quite decided who I want to be."

"If I may correct you—"

"Certainly."

She caught sight of a set of double doors that led to the library. They stretched almost to the ceiling and arched at the top like a cathedral entrance.

"I don't know if you noticed, but society today tends to define who we are by what we do. Although our occupation consumes much of our waking moments, it is still only an occupation or career, if you will. It is more likely today then it was when I was younger that one will change career direction. If a gentleman says he is a lawyer and suddenly finds himself without the ability to practice law, he then states "he was a lawyer." I don't know about you, but even at 85 years old, I don't want to refer to myself as 'used to be'

when 'I still am'. Jannie chuckled. Mr. Sherman had certainly demonstrated he wasn't a has-been.

"Let me tell you how I came to this realization. One winter when our family was ice skating, my oldest son tripped and put his hands out in front of him to break his fall. Our second oldest, who was right beside him, couldn't move out of the way quickly enough and ran over his brother's fingers with his skate. The father of one of their friends was standing on the sidelines and quickly bandaged our son's fingers. By the time we arrived, our son was sitting quietly on the bench with his hand all wrapped up. I joked that our friend was proficient at first aid because his wife is a doctor. He was quick to declare if his wife were here, she would say that is not 'who she is'; it is just 'what she does'. He went on to tell us that she never tells people she is a doctor, but rather when asked, she responds by saying she works in the medical field. She even goes so far as to have the bank print Mrs. on her personal cheques instead of Dr. in front of her name. In essence, she doesn't allow her occupation to define who she is."

Derek had seen she needed a mentor and, oddly enough, Mr. Sherman seemed to perfectly fit the bill.

"Hmmm," Jannie mused. "I can't say that I ever thought about it like that before."

Suddenly, Jannie knew why she was here. Her initial thoughts were of helping an older gentleman transition to a life without his companion, but she realized this would be for her benefit as much as his. Derek had seen she needed a mentor and, oddly enough, Mr. Sherman seemed to perfectly fit the bill.

Mr. Sherman's words broke into her thoughts. "When we define people according their occupation, we subconsciously categorize them in a social class. Some people are defined by their jobs or career, others by their talents. Some are defined by inabilities like being confined to a wheelchair. Too many times, people are defined by their money or lack of it. Sadly, we elevate those with much monetary assets and ignore those with character and morality. By the way, money can be lost or gained in a single moment; good character traits and morality, however, are the result of a lifetime of growth coupled with applied wisdom and maturity. Many times, those who come into wealth overnight end up losing if because they lack the inner qualities that precipitate the good decision making necessary to retain it."

"Other people are defined by their possessions—the one with the lavish sports car, the huge estate or the successful business. Until we can define ourselves by the goodness in our hearts, especially that which is governed by the Holy Spirit, we do not have the true definition of who we are."

"No wonder so many people suffer from identity crisis. They are looking to the outside, not the inside to determine who they are."

"Exactly. You will begin to recognize emotionally healthy people when you see that their occupation and possessions are simply by-products of their character, not the sum representation of their being."

When Jannie got home that evening, she pulled out a notebook from within her pile of textbooks. She began to make notes from the conversation she had with Mr. Sherman. This man, no doubt, had a wealth of insight, and she was not about to let any of it be forgotten.

CHAPTER 3

JANNIE PULLED UP TO THE RESTAURANT AND glanced around the parking lot for familiar faces. When she found no one she recognized, she walked inside the building where she was greeted by a smiling employee holding a menu.

"For one?"

"No, I am looking for the ladies group—"

"Right this way."

Jannie followed the server through rows of guest-filled tables to a set of huge doors at the back of the restaurant. As the server held open one of the black wooden doors, Jannie spied Raquel, the girl who had invited her to the meeting. She slid into the chair next to Raquel as the speaker took the podium.

"Good evening, ladies. Thank you for the privilege of sharing with you tonight. I call this talk "The heart of the matter." The clanking of the cutlery on the dishes grew silent as the ladies focussed their attention to the front of the room. The speaker seemed mostly confident, but her voice held a slight hesitation in it—almost as if she was unsure of how her message would be received.

"I look around and see people in my family struggling with issues, and many of my friends have issues. And churches have issues. And the thing is, especially in my case, I've had the same issue for decades and have tried many different ways to correct it. Sometimes, I have a bit of a breakthrough, but then it seems to manifest in a slightly different area. I then have to stop and admit this isn't working. I must be missing something."

"When I was in college, I had a professor tell me something very profound. He said that trying to solve a problem by treating the symptoms is like trying to cure pneumonia with a box of facial tissues. Essentially, we are neglecting to find the cause of the problem and curing it at the root.

It's not the intellectual knowledge of the matter that brings freedom, but rather the experiential knowing.

Although this nugget of wisdom stuck with me all these years, I didn't fully comprehend its significance. Therefore, I didn't put it into practice. The Bible says you shall know the truth, and the truth shall make you free. But it's not the intellectual knowledge of the matter that brings freedom, but rather the experiential knowing. In other words, it is the application and subsequent manifestation of knowledge in our lives that frees us. You can know someone on a casual basis, or you can have an intimate relationship with that person. Two different things.

"When it comes to many of the issues that go unresolved, it is often because we can only see the symptoms and mistake them for the actual problem. We focus all our efforts on resolving the symptoms when what we really need to do is identify the root problem and resolve it at its origin. As a result of attacking the source, the symptoms will eventually dissolve. Many issues—whether they show up as physical ailments, relationship problems, or financial lack—are rooted in the heart. They require healing at a heart level before the symptoms will ever go away.

"In Luke 4, Jesus said He was sent to heal the broken hearted and set at liberty those who are bruised or crushed or shattered. He says to set free those who have been wounded or hurt. That means that wounds suffered in the past can hold people in bondage. Unfortunately, in today's world, we often dismiss emotional healing altogether. We think because internal issues aren't visible, they just go away. But time does NOT heal; it simply distances you from the initial pain. And you can't 'just get over it'. In the physical realm, we don't go to the doctor with blood squirting out of us and have him say, "just get over it." It's no less real in the area of the heart. We have a stereotypical view of a psychiatrist sitting cross legged with notepad in hand while the patient is lying on the couch, pouring out his problems. While emotional healing does begin with recognizing we have an issue and desiring to resolve it, the situation doesn't stop there.

Time does NOT heal; it simply distances you from the initial pain. And you can't 'just get over it'.

"I'm not suggesting we have to relive or undo the past. The past is just that. BUT if something hurt you in the past and you didn't get set free from the pain or the influence of it, you will suffer the effects of it until you get healed or die, whichever comes first. I'm not advising we dwell on pain. I simply want us to acknowledge we all get hurt in life, and we need to be taught what to do about it. I don't know about you, but I don't remember a class called "Pain Management 101." Since we aren't taught how to eliminate emotional pain, we use default methods to deal with it. Mostly, it's denial or suppression. According to marriage counsellor and author Jimmy Evans, we use three main ways of coping to deal with pain (https://www.rightnow.org/Content/Series/482). The first is to 'motivate,' which simply means we spend an unhealthy amount of energy working, so we don't have time to feel our pain. The second is what he calls 'meditating'. This is dwelling on the painful situation and rehearsing it again and again until it takes over our lives. The third coping mechanism is 'to medicate', which is quite obvious and has become a huge issue in our society. People who are hurting use drugs, alcohol, pornography or any other 'medication' they can find to ease the pain in their hearts."

Jannie shifted in her chair. She took a few bites of her meal, trying to be as quiet as she could while focussing on the speaker's words.

"I knew a family of children," the woman continued, "who lost their mom at an early age. Each reacted differently. One went on to receive the highest level of education in his field but couldn't hold on to a relationship. Another became a workaholic at the expense of his family. The third child became homeless, fought alcoholism and, although he possessed a brilliant mind, never held a steady job. I believe each suffered from abandonment issues. None of them, however, were offered counselling and never received the healing they so badly craved.

"Since I discovered this, it seems every time I come across a new book or hear a new speaker, they echo the same theme—getting to the root of an issue and healing it at the heart level. Again, I don't want to focus on pain, but so many of us struggle for decades with issues we just can't figure out how to fix. There must be a solution, but why is it so elusive? We often turn to the church community, but many times we have not received the necessary help.

"What is wrong with many churches today? It seems they are taking an extreme route of denial in the body of Christ and are becoming like the flock in Ezekiel 34.

"The weak you have not strengthened, nor have you healed those who were sick, nor bound up the broken, nor brought back what was driven away, nor sought what was lost; but with force and cruelty you have ruled them. So they were scattered because there was no shepherd; and they became food for all the beasts of the field when they were scattered. My sheep wandered through all the mountains, and on every high hill; yes, My flock was scattered over the whole face of the earth, and no one was seeking or searching for them." (Ezekiel 34:4–6 NKJV)

"God, our good shepherd, has put shepherds over His flocks. They may be spiritual leaders in the church, or they may be heads of homes. Unfortunately, many of the leaders are not trained in issues of the heart. Even more have issues of their own that remain unhealed. If the heart issues go unhealed, the flock gets scattered and they become vulnerable to prey.

"If you have had your feelings hurt, the church might say, 'oh, you're a Christian, just get over it'. But there are Christians who have been saved for more than 50 years, and they haven't 'gotten over it', whatever 'it' is. Oh, they've ignored it, suppressed it, or pretended it never happened, but the second that issue gets touched, the manifestation of the hurt feelings come out in one form or another. It can be offence, control, domination, suppression—you name it, but it all stems from the hurt they were told to 'just get over it'. No, get it healed! Nothing in Christianity is automatic. You may have such a dynamic conversion experience that you lay out all your hurts at the altar the first day. You may allow Jesus to bathe you in so much of his love that you receive an enormous amount of healing right then and there. But that is not the norm. Usually, after we say the prayer of salvation, we still experience a lot of unhealed hurt and a lot of bondage from which we need to be set free and ignorance to overcome.

"Beware of the blanket statement that you need to get into the Word. Rest assured that if you want to get to know God better, you must read the Bible. But how are you reading it? Is it to understand? A 1982 song performed by the Gaither Vocal Band said,"I was glad when I heard you're getting into the Word, but is the Word getting into you?" You can spend hours memorizing Scripture, but if you are just accumulating information, it does nothing more than when the Bible was sitting on the coffee table. The life is in the Word and Jesus is called the Word, but it is the power that backs the Word that can bring about change and transformation."

The room was silent. This was weighty material the speaker was dishing out. Jannie didn't want to look at anyone directly but sensed that most of the women were attentively sober, waiting for what the next few minutes would divulge.

"I'm not an expert in healing of the heart," continued the speaker. "I hope someday to get there. All I know is I'm on a quest to have all heart issues healed, starting with me and then my family and then the Church. I believe we can all be conquerors now and not have to wait for someday to get it all together. There are excellent source materials out there. At the end of the presentation, I will hand out a list of books and websites you may investigate. All I want to do tonight is to get you to look at fruit. Begin to ask yourself questions like 'why am I always irritated with this or why am I always struggling with that?' Once you realize there is a root and begin to seek healing at the root level—which is the heart—I believe you will see change in the fruit.

You can spend hours memorizing Scripture, but if you are just accumulating information, it does nothing more than when the Bible was sitting on the coffee table.

"I hope this will incite you to begin your own journey to healing and to go on to become the victorious woman whom God designed you to be." *(Author's Note: see Resources section at the end of this book.)*

A spontaneous round of applause burst in the room as the speaker took her seat near the podium. The silence broken, the ladies began to chatter among themselves. Raquel leaned over to Jannie with inquisitive eyes and whispered.

"What did you think?

"Wow, that was pretty profound," said Jannie. "I might have to meditate on that for awhile."

Raquel chuckled, "Yes, I feel the same way."

Problems have a root. Most of the time, we don't know the root, so we attempt to treat the symptoms that we see with our eyes, which is just the fruit of the problem.

The two ladies said their goodbyes and made their way out of the restaurant. As Jannie drove home, she thought of the fateful day she ran into Derek at the coffee shop. It had only been a month since then, but she had learned so much more in these few short weeks than she had in college during the past year and a half. She figured it was time to give Derek a call.

"Sure, I'd love to catch up," said Derek cheerfully. "How about an early dinner at the pizza parlor on 22nd? I can meet you there about 5 p.m."

This time the weather was warm and the sky was bright. They decided to take a seat on the back patio away from the noise inside the popular pizzeria.

"So, tell me what has transpired since we last spoke." Derek's voice was inviting, and he focused his full attention on Jannie as if she were the only person in the place.

"I've got to say, Mr. Sherman is a dear. I had no idea what I was getting into when I agreed to have tea with him, but I feel this was something that was meant to be. He has such wisdom."

"I knew you two would hit it off." Derek was grinning from ear to ear, still intently fixed on Jannie. His eyes danced with pleasure at the news.

"I sure am learning a lot in a very short time. That reminds me, the other night I went with my friend Raquel to a church ladies get-together, and the speaker touched on a very interesting topic. She talked about how issues or problems have a root. Most of the time, we don't know the root, so we attempt to treat the symptoms that we see with our eyes, which is just the fruit of the problem. I can see it now since she identified it. I know tons of people who go through their whole life putting out fires, but they never seem to get to a place where the fires are less frequent. Now I see they are treating symptoms and never getting to the root. I don't get why so many people just never see it. It's so simple. Are we that stupid or is this not taught in mainstream?"

"Well," Derek interjected, "it's probably because we were never trained to see anything other than face value. If you can't see it with your eyes, it doesn't exist, right? Just like germs."

"Germs? That's an interesting analogy," stated Jannie.

"Not too many centuries ago, a doctor would be considered a quack if he washed his hands between patients," Derek continued. "Colleagues would scoff at anyone who thought there were little bugs crawling around making people sick. If you can't see them, they must not be there, right?"

"Yeah, and the world is flat."

Jannie took a bite of pizza. She already felt a lot less uptight about her life than she had in the coffee shop. A break from college at this point was the right decision for her.

"I looked up some of the resources the speaker mentioned the other night. It's really quite enlightening. I made some notes." Jannie pulled out the notebook in which she had begun to record her thoughts.

Derek sat back ready to listen to her read. She marvelled at how easily she could talk to him without feeling any fear.

"The catch 22 is this," Jannie began. "We suffer a hurt, and since we aren't taught how to deal with pain, we bury that hurt. Unfortunately, that hardens our heart and prevents us from resolving the pain—or should I say the source of the pain. Then we begin to lose our perspective. That, in turn, disables us from being able to look objectively into the real issue. We almost always need a third party to recognize the problem. Sadly, though, when others try to point out issues that we need to deal with, we just take them as a personal attack against us. So the hurts not dealt with cause more pain and the cycle continues."

Jannie looked up to gauge Derek's reaction.

"If that's the case," he said, "I sure do know a lot of people who live out of their hurt."

CHAPTER 4

SOMEWHERE IN THE DISTANCE, A LAWNMOWER hummed. Birds carried on happy conversations, oblivious to everything else around them. The sudden noise of a jet plane shot through the air. Through a half opened eye, Jannie focused on the bedroom clock: 2:07 p.m. She rolled over, swung her feet onto the floor, and sat looking out the window. From the edge of the bed, she could see the neighbor's cat stretched out across cool cement in the shade of a gangly over-grown walnut tree. A light breeze touched the cylinders of the wind chimes hanging above the patio table. They tinkled melodically as if on cue. It was not usual for Jannie to have a nap in the afternoon. She must have been drained. Slowly she recounted the events of the past two days in her mind. She shifted her attention to her thoughts to recall the memory of her brother's visit. Ed had arrived unexpectedly on Friday evening just as she and her parents were sitting down to dinner. All excited about a new job offer, he had not taken the time to call. Instead, he had gathered most of his belongings, thrown them into the back of his convertible, and headed to the eastern part of the country. He probably wouldn't have stopped had they not been on the way, thought Jannie. The next day and a half was filled with sorting his things, leaving some in boxes in the basement, and digging through keepsakes he had left behind when he went off to college five years previously. Jannie had missed her late night talks with Ed. Almost four years older than Jannie, his life experiences were always just a jump ahead of hers. She liked the idea she could live some his escapades through his oral essays. This way, she could be involved without actually experiencing the trauma that accompanied many of his antics. Ed was not the troublemaker their father liked to portray him to be, but he was definitely less conservative than she. He always seemed to be on an adventure.

Excitement shot through her like a jolt of electricity. Tomorrow was Monday and she would see Mr. Sherman. She could hardly wait to tell him of her discovery.

"This is it, Jannie. This is the break I have been waiting for. If this pans out, the four years of college will have all been worth it. That—and I will be able to pay off all my student loans in barely more than a year."

The entire weekend had been consumed with Ed. Other plans had either been put on hold or simply forgotten. Then, just as quickly as he arrived, he was gone.

Jannie stumbled into the kitchen. It seemed so empty since Ed had left earlier that day. He had a way of making his presence known wherever he was; this house was no exception. As she poured herself a fresh cup of coffee, revelation struck. The thought had not made its way to her consciousness until now. She had caught a glimpse of the long scar on his left leg as he climbed into his car and waved one last goodbye. She had seen it numerous times before, but it was not until this moment that the significance of it hit her. Excitement shot through her like a jolt of electricity. Tomorrow was Monday and she would see Mr. Sherman. She could hardly wait to tell him of her discovery.

Monday morning, Jannie awoke early and got ready before any-one else came down for breakfast.

"Where are you off to so early this morning?" Dad appeared at the kitchen door just as she was finishing her last bite of toast.

"I have a few errands to run before I go see Mr. Sherman today. I also want to see if I can get a book he keeps talking about. He has a copy in his library, but I don't want to ask him if I can bor-row it. I am sure I can find one at a second-hand store."

"Sounds good. It never hurts to read more books." He flashed her a smile that was part encouragement and part jab. He had al-ways made sure she and Ed had access to any book they wanted. "Oh, by the way, Ed called just after you went to bed last night. He made it to Durlinton last night. He is supposed to meet with his new boss later this morning. Thought you'd like to know."

"Thanks, Dad. Gotta run. See you later tonight."

When Jannie arrived at Mr. Sherman's later that day, he was not there to greet her as usual.

"Mr. Sherman is on a telephone call overseas," announced Ms. Brookes. "Would you like to wait for him in the library?"

"Oh, certainly," Jannie said, her voice full of excitement.

"I will get the sweets," said Ms. Brookes and headed to the op-posite end of the house. Jannie studied the hallway intently this time, noting every little detail as she went. Artwork lined both sides of the wide passage. Although the frames were of similar style and colour, they each housed a different style of art. Some were portraits. Others scenery. The most intriguing one was of a young boy. If authentic, it could have been from the Victorian era. His clothing resembled what she thought to be schoolboy fashion. The collar on his shirt was tightly closed around his neck with a small bowtie clasped beneath it. He sat rigid on an ornate chair with no hint of smile on his face. It was not clear to Jannie if it was a painting or an old photograph. The monochromatic image suggested it could be either. She paused and studied it for a moment before proceeding through the double doors. Could it be Mr. Sherman as a child? Or even his father, perhaps?

The library was particularly inviting today. Light streamed through the window, making the room feel bright and warm despite the fact it was lined with dark cherry coloured wood on three walls. There was every type of book imaginable: hardcover, softcover, cloth-bound. Huge leather covered encyclopedias were poised against the east wall, flanked by brass bookends that one might only see in an antique store. The room itself was even larger than the used bookstore she had visited earlier that day, but it lacked the usual mustiness of a library, a testament to the cleaning abilities of Ms. Brookes, no doubt.

"I have been collecting books since I was nine years old." Mr. Sherman appeared at the entrance door, cane in hand.

"That's an impressive collection, I must say," remarked Jannie, still gazing at the volumes of accumulated information.

"I used to be a hoarder of books when I was younger," he chuckled, making his way to the small round table at the window. "It must have been due to an upbringing in which books were scarce. Then I realized the material was not just for me, but it could enhance the lives of those around me. That's when I began to buy multiple copies of certain works I deemed valuable and give them out to people as I saw fit. Planting seed, I guess you could call it." Again he chuckled as he lowered himself into the comfortable leather chair. "With all these electronic gadgets that can hold vast amounts of knowledge in a single device, I still prefer the look and feel of a well constructed book."

"I agree with you." Jannie thought of the limited selection of textbooks and novels that filled a small bookshelf in her room. She determined she would increase her collection sooner than later.

"So, you had a visit from your brother, Ed?" By now Mr. Sherman was well acquainted with the dynamics of Jannie's family and the many activities that were apt to happen on any given occasion.

"News travels fast. Did Derek tell you?"

"Yes, he was by here yesterday afternoon for a quick visit."

Derek had made friends with Ed during the times he came by the house to see Jannie. It was not unusual for him to make an appearance when Ed was in town. Always up for a social occasion, Derek made a point of stopping by to see Mr. Sherman whenever he was in the neighborhood. Mr. Sherman was always ready for company, so the two were a good match.

Jannie looked out over the beautiful garden she loved to admire, then turned to Mr. Sherman with a quick smile and offered him the plate of sweets.

He raised an eyebrow and looked at her intently.

"You seem eager to share something with me. What is it, my dear?"

There was every type of book imaginable: hardcover, softcover, clothbound. Huge leather covered encyclopedias were poised against the east wall, flanked by brass bookends that one might only see in an antique store.

Jannie paused, somewhat amazed at how easily Mr. Sherman could read her after only a few months of getting to know each other.

"Well, the other day, I had a revelation," she began. "Let me give you a bit of background first. "

About six years ago, my brother suffered a serious leg injury. It happened while he was working with a renovation company fixing the inside of a garage. There was a ladder leaned up against a wall, and he climbed it to where his feet were about 4 feet above the ground. All of a sudden, without warning, the ladder slipped and slid down the wall with him on it. He held on and road it down, but when it hit the ground, his left leg went through the bottom rung to the floor. The rung had a serrated edge and, consequently, ripped his shin open between his ankle and his knee. He was taken immediately to the local hospital about 15 minutes from the jobsite where it was cleaned up and stitches were applied. Over the course of the next several weeks, the wound healed over and nothing was left but a scar. Normally, that would have been the end of the story. But few months went by and something was wrong. Even though the leg was visibly healed on the outside, infection had set in under the scar tissue and it began to fester. One afternoon, in pain, he drove to a larger hospital in a city about 90 minutes away. At this point, doctors had to reopen the wound and remove all the underlying infection that was dangerously close to the bone. They told him that had he left it untreated any longer,

> When it hit the ground, his left leg went through the bottom rung to the floor. The rung had a serrated edge and, consequently, ripped his shin open between his ankle and his knee.

he would have lost his leg. He's fine now and has a scar I am sure he hardly notices.

"Yesterday, it hit me, though. This is the perfect analogy. Life dishes out disappointments and hurts—some through tragedy or abuse—but each of us has had his or her heart broken to some degree. When we cover up or bury the hurt, the poison begins to fester in our hearts and serious consequences can result."

Mr. Sherman sat silently for a moment pondering Jannie's statements. "That is very observant, my friend. You are wise beyond your years. And you are right. The problem is not that we get hurt; the problem begins when those hurts are not dealt with. It's up to us, though, to recognize them and to take action to get our heart wounds healed. I'm not saying we can do this entirely by ourselves. But we have to take the initial steps. If we don't call for help, no one is going to come running to find the cure for us. In my opinion, the most tragic of heart issue is denial. How can we get healed if we do not acknowledge we have a problem?

Jannie's gaze seemed to be focussed on the scenery in front of her, but she saw none of it. Instead, her mind's eye was reconstructing vivid scenes from her past. Why, she wondered, had she reacted in such a manner to a seemingly minor incident when other times, a more serious situation garnered little to no reaction at all? Could this be what much of the world was missing? Continually putting out fires but not knowing what is causing the blaze? This definitely needed more contemplation. Jannie excused herself with promises to continue this vein of conversation in a few days. Mr. Sherman agreed they had not yet solved all the world's problems. Jannie chuckled at how lightly he could make a very serious subject.

That night, Jannie surveyed the moon as it shone like a spotlight onto the sleepy town. Almost a complete circle, the oversized orange ball cast a beam onto the water cutting a path from one side of the lake to the other. From where she sat perched by the third floor window, she observed the rows of lights that dotted the hills on the other side of the inlet. She snuggled into her thick down-filled comforter and drew in the cool air from the open window. It was very refreshing. It was easy to think clearly on a night like this—no outside stimulation to disturb her. The only sound was that of an owl in the distant trees. She closed her eyes and consciously began to move away from thinking too hard and turned her attention to what was inside her heart. What was it saying? What could she perceive from within it?

Mr. Sherman knew a lot more about the subject of the heart than it first appeared—most likely from first-hand accounts.

She recounted the conversation from earlier in the day and concluded that Mr. Sherman knew a lot more about the subject of the heart than it first appeared—most likely from first-hand accounts. Maybe he was right. Maybe the best lessons ARE learned through experience and not from books. The lessons that stick with us are the ones we learn with our hearts. At his age, one would expect Mr. Sherman to be, at the very least, somewhat cynical, harboring some amount of bitterness—about something! Surely he could not have made it all these years without suffering a degree of heartbreak. But how did he come to this point in his life without the evidence of baggage? What was his secret? He definitely had insight. What she really needed to find out was how to go about getting one's heart healed. She was sure he knew.

CHAPTER 5

THE AFTERNOON STARTED OUT IN THE USUAL way—Jannie and Mr. Sherman sharing conversation over a cup of tea and a pastry. They found they had similar tastes in sweets, which made it easy for Ms. Brookes to supply an endless array of baked goods. On this particular afternoon, the conversation was exceptionally trivial, and Mr. Sherman seemed a bit distant. It was not in a bad way, just a reflective manner like he was carefully constructing his speech to find just the right words.

"Jannie," he began, "I want to convey to you a matter of heart issues. The simple reason is I have had first-hand experience in a certain matter having observed it unfold from close proximity. The outcome was rather painful to watch, and if I can prevent the painful experience from happening to one other person, then I will consider my life to be a success."

"One of the great qualities of human beings is the ability to learn lessons from others' achievements and mistakes. It is as if our brains can enter a simulation mode that allows us to emulate what is happening in a given circumstance. By reading or observing, we can learn the outcome without having to actually experience the situation ourselves.

"You are a young woman, finding her way in the world—no doubt having to fight off would-be suitors in the hopes of one day finding a partner with whom to share your life. There is a lot of advice out there about what to look for and what to avoid in a man. Most of what I have read or seen, however, focuses mainly on the outside and fails to decipher the underlying motivations or causes of behaviours. Remember when we discussed the ideas of roots and fruits?"

Life is about perception, but we need to be cautious because sometimes we make decisions based on what we identify with our physical senses rather than what we discern in our hearts.

"Of course. That cleared up a lot of misconceptions for me," said Jannie, listening intently to what Mr. Sherman was about to reveal.

"A good phrase to remember is 'things are not always as they seem'. Life is about perception, but we need to be cautious because sometimes we make decisions based on what we identify with our physical senses rather than what we discern in our hearts. My brother-in-law used to say, 'Reality is just the collective hallucination of the masses'. While I believe there is some truth to that statement, I don't hold it as 100% true, but that's a completely different topic. One for another day, I am sure."

Mr. Sherman smiled and took a sip of tea. There was a brief silence as if he were formulating the next portion of his dissertation.

"To me, with each generation, our society is becoming increasingly distant from our moral roots. As traditional family values rapidly erode before our eyes, I believe the struggle to find a 'decent boy' to share your life with is becoming even more difficult. Men are no longer raising healthy male offspring. Sometimes, a couple of generations have come and gone with no father figure in the household. Also, the family unit has become so dysfunctional that the male figurehead doesn't know what it is like to be a real father. Thus we have a society full of 'little boys' trying to function in a world that requires emotional and psychological maturity."

Jannie sat forward, attentive to Mr. Sherman's every word, wondering what revelation he was about to disclose.

"Let me tell you the story of Olive. She was a good friend of my wife's for years, both having grown up in the same community and having attended the same high school. Over the course of our marriage, Olive became a good friend of our family and often spent special occasions with us because her family was now quite far away. She spoke of her life in great detail because, as my brother had observed, she wore her heart on her sleeve. We always knew of the latest aspiring boyfriend and made many interventions in order to steer her away from making a mistake. Many came and went in her life as she clung to the romantic concept that, one day, prince charming would materialize and sweep her off her feet. We all felt sure we would recognize him when he appeared.

"What probably seemed like an eternity to her, he showed up. He seemed like the nicest man. For a few weeks, he focused totally on her, taking her out to places she enjoyed, buying flowers and treats, and becoming involved in the smallest details of her life. After only three months of dating, he proposed; she was ready. This had been the man she had been waiting for as long as she could remember.

"After a few months, our contact with Olive diminished. What we thought would be an integration of this newfound member into our family actually turned out to be the opposite. Soon, much of Olive's life revolved around her husband, his interests, his job, his life. We lost contact except for the occasional pleasantry exchanged at church. Something had gone wrong.

"My wife had observed that Olive was distant and guarded. The vibrancy we had seen and experienced from her was all but gone. Our hearts hurt for her.

"Then one day, as suddenly as she had disappeared, she showed up at our door, alone and wanting to talk. Over the next few weeks, over coffee and sometimes into the late evening, she unveiled tales of what went on behind closed doors.

"It took me many months of research and much musing before I came to a conclusion. Turns out he had all the attributes of a misogynist."

"A what?" asked Jannie.

"A misogynist. It's just a fancy word for woman hater."

"But if he hated women, why did she marry him? Wait, if he hated women, why would he want to get married in the first place?" continued Jannie.

"That's the thing with misogyny. The characteristics are not that blatantly obvious that they stem from hatred. Proverbs 26:24 says, 'A hateful person disguises himself with his speech and harbors deceit within' (Holman Christian Standard Bible). That's why it is hard to diagnose at first. Many of the signs are deceiving. For instance, misogynists generally want to get married because they fear it might appear that something is wrong with them if they were not married. The other thing is misogynists are not born—they are made. What was probably the case with this man is he had suffered a traumatic experience in his life from a female in authority. This caused him to have an inner drive to destroy women. He only needed to destroy one. None of this was at a conscious level, of course. But still, it was the perfect case. He married a woman and used his authority to make her submit. The things he asked her to submit to were not necessarily legally or morally correct; they were just his idea of what he thought should be. But since no outward physical signs of abuse were evident, he seemed to get away with it. Not that he did it consciously, but a careful examination of his life revealed traits that were textbook accurate.

"Misogyny is dangerous because the afflicted person acts out of a subconscious that is laced with fear, hurt and anger. If he could have come to the point of asking for help, he could have been healed. Sadly, though, he remained that way until the day he died. Even more sad were the lives he negatively affected."

Misogyny is dangerous because the afflicted person acts out of a subconscious that is laced with fear, hurt and anger.

"What happened to Olive?"

"Eventually, she left him and filed for divorce," answered Mr. Sherman.

"Wait a minute, isn't divorce frowned upon in the church?"

"Oh yes, but I believe much of the church is under the deception of what divorce really is and what it means to God. And it is most likely from a mistranslation of Scripture. Not a misinterpretation but an actual incident in which the true meaning is lost in translation. We all quote 'God hates divorce' and add the connotation that, therefore, God hates those who are divorced. But did you know that God himself was divorced?"

Jannie shot him a look of disbelief.

"I didn't think so," he said. "But it is plainly written in Jeremiah 3:8. What is not plain to our western English minds is that in the original language, God speaks about two distinct concepts—the first is divorce, which referred to the legal dissolution of the marriage with a certificate, like the one Moses issued. The second is "putting away," which is foreign to our western culture. In the original language, 'putting away' was a distinct term. The early Church understood this because its people knew the language. What God hates is the act of 'putting away' of one spouse by the other. Let's just use the example of a husband putting away his wife. In some cases, he would act in such a manner as to cause her to leave. This was often done using anger and aggression to control her or make her feel unwanted or unworthy. In other cases, the husband would physically put his wife out of the house. Because women were not allowed to work in those days, the wife would be forced to live with another man who would support her, or she supported herself through prostitution. This of course made her the adulterer. What society saw was a woman no longer living with her husband and, therefore, committing adultery through her new living situation. What society didn't see is how she was mistreated to the point of death, even if only death of the soul. The husband would then return to the synagog and receive the pity of all who saw him—all the while he was the perpetrator of the wrongdoing and that was what God hated.

What God hates is the act of 'putting away' of one spouse by the other.

"It spills over into the New Testament as well—the mistranslation, I mean. You see, we don't have a separate word for 'putting away' in our language, so it is all lumped under the word 'divorce'. This becomes really confusing in Mark 10:11 where Jesus says if you divorce your wife, she becomes an adulterer. Correctly translated, he is saying if you put her away WITHOUT a proper legal certificate of divorce, it is an adulterous situation.

This is where generations of churchgoers have been duped and have caused all kinds of wrong accusations. God hates the act of putting away that caused the other party to eventually get a certificate of divorce. Divorce itself, is not a sin or God wouldn't have divorced Israel. He did so because she FIRST put him away. In my opinion, the sin lies in the condemnation dished out by the Church. But don't take my word for it only; look it up for yourself."

Jannie could hardly wait to get home that afternoon. It was no reflection on Mr. Sherman at all. No, she loved every minute of her time spent with him. Today, however, felt like she had happened upon an entirely new world. In her room, she opened a new browser window on her computer and typed in the keyword 'misogynist'. There it was on www.lifeskillsintl.org/Men_Who_Hate_Women.html. She opened the link without hesitation. Wow! Who knew? All the traits Mr. Sherman had alluded to and more. Many of the characteristics seemed so positive that it was almost hard to believe they had such devastating effects on others. Jannie sat back in her chair for a moment and reflected. All this information coming to her—what did it mean? What was she supposed to do with it?

"Jannie, you home?" Her mother was calling from the bottom of the stairs.

"Be right down, Mom." It was nice not having to move out of her parents' home to go to college, but it was also annoying. Unlike her brother who had moved to another city to further his education, she chose to stay home and go to a local school. It made it as convenient for her parents as it did her. They could delay the transition from teenager to full adult while Jannie was left to struggle with what her role in the household actually was. Today, it was probably errand girl.

"Jannie, can I get you to drop this off at the post box when you go out? I was back in the driveway before I remembered I was supposed to mail it."

Called it. Oh well, small price to pay for being able to stay with them. Both her parents had been exceptionally casual about her taking a semester off. They had been very supportive, even though she said she wouldn't be actively seeking a job. At this point, they were just concerned that she knew the direction she was supposed to take for her life and not spend more time pursuing something she may regret later.

Back in her room, Jannie skimmed through the pile of papers she needed to complete to resume her college studies. It was getting close to the point where she would have to submit the forms in order to return the next semester. A page flipped open and caught her eye. "Degree Requirements" was the heading at the top of the page. Her eye followed the highlighted phrases until it rested on "Thesis."

"The student must submit a document in support of candidature in order to receive his or her academic degree. The written dissertation must present the author's own research and findings…" Many times throughout the last semester, she had anxiety about the seemingly daunting task. Because her thesis was in the distant future, she was less intimidated by the thought of completing it. She wondered if spending time with Mr. Sherman was actually changing her perspective on life. It sure wasn't hurting.

The weekend was fast approaching, and Mom was thinking out loud about what to cook for dinner. Ed was coming home, so there would be a family meal on Saturday evening. Jannie stopped her at pot roast.

"Can't we just have a normal roast of beef?" asked Jannie.

"I thought you liked pot roast?

"Yeah, kind of, but you know Derek is going to come over. Whether Ed calls him or he happens by or he talks to Mr. Sherman, you can count on Derek being here, so we might as well have something a little less 'homey,'" concluded Jannie.

"Sure, we can have the full meal deal. I don't mind. We will pretend it is Thanksgiving or a Sunday afternoon meal when our pastor is usually invited."

"I hardly think Ed or Derek are pastor material but, yeah, that's what I meant," said Jannie.

And so, when Saturday night dinner rolled around, Mom had seen to every detail. Normally, she wasn't a very good cook. She struggled with the day-to-day chore of providing a meal. Often, it ended up being a build-your-own burger or a can of something with bread. When it came to entertaining, though, it was a totally different story. She would pull out every gadget and obscure dish that maybe only saw the light of day once a year. She set the table in grand fashion with a crisply ironed tablecloth and napkins to match. The food was served on platters with silver trimmed edges, and the serving spoons came from the middle drawer in the china cabinet, which no one dared to touch.

At this point, they were just concerned that she knew the direction she was supposed to take for her life and not spend more time pursuing something she may regret later.

When they were seated, they were all present. Derek was there as predicted. Jannie secretly felt the family was not complete without him.

After dinner, everyone took something into the kitchen, and the light conversation continued while coffee was brewing. Dessert would be delayed for at least a half hour. Ed and Derek were the first to go off to the living room.

"You know that girl Monica I told you of earlier? Ed began. "I thought I'd take her to a seaside restaurant for a first date."

"Is it a really expensive place?" Derek wondered.

"Very nice. I want to dazzle her right from the start. That should score a few points right off the bat, don't you think?"

"Guys, there is no point system." Dad walked in from the kitchen with a glass of coke in his hand and sat down in his favourite chair in the corner of the room. Ed turned his head quickly, obviously unaware that Dad had been listening.

"But that's what all the dating sites say," replied Ed.

When acceptance or rejection is BASED solely on performance, something is wrong. What is employed here is emotional manipulation.

"Well, Ed, I have been married more decades than I was single. I can tell you they are wrong. I mean, many guys maneuver that way, thinking if they do something for their significant other, then surely they should be rewarded. But in the end, they are the losers. And you know why? Because a point system perpetuates and works solely off the dysfunction of a performance-based relationship, which is no relationship. Performance-based relationships are doomed to fail because they lead to acceptance based on performance. The key word is acceptance. Yes, when you are asked to do a job or complete a task, if your heart is right, you will do it to the best of your ability. That is not what I'm referring to. When acceptance or rejection is BASED solely on performance, something is wrong. What is employed here is emotional manipulation. 'You didn't do what I wanted you to do, so now I'm angry or hurt'. Or 'You did what I wanted you to do, so you will be rewarded (with points!)'. It's like training a dog."

Ed looked at the cat sprawled at Dad's feet. He leaned toward it, rubbing his hands in an engaging motion. "Here, Fido," he called in an elevated tone of voice.

"Ed," Jannie scolded from the doorway. "She's not a dog!"

Derek chuckled, "See, even the cat gets it."

Dad took over the conversation again, oblivious to Ed's humorous intervention.

"When a relationship is based on performance, it becomes about what you do, NOT who you are. Acceptance or rejection of a person based on performance is anti gospel, anti Christ. Our salvation was never deserved. Jesus offered it to each man, no matter the calibre or degree of sin. This is because God loves everyone, without exception. (John 3:16) There is, however, a difference between being loved by God and pleasing Him. Hebrews 11:6 states that we can't please Him if we don't use faith. In performance-based relationships, the two get all mixed up. By our actions, we subconsciously say to the other person that our love for him or her is based solely on that person's performance. Here's the irony: if you love people for WHO THEY ARE—not 'what they do' or don't do—the acceptance they feel will result in them willingly 'doing' anything for you! By focussing on their worth as a person, they will want to be around you and spend time with you. They will desire to please you and do things with you. When you access the heart, then the 'doing' will be heartfelt. It will be genuine and not done out of obligation or duty."

"Wow, Dad. You should be a psychologist or a therapist or at least a preacher. Yeah, you should preach, Dad. That was really good." That said, Ed began his own round of his applause. Dad was not overly amused but Derek laughed. Ed always seemed to be able to say the things everyone else was thinking but were too polite to say. And he always got away with it.

Jannie appeared in the doorway.

"No wonder you don't have a girlfriend, Ed. You've been going about it all wrong."

This time Derek laughed heartily. "That's what I love about this family," he said. "You guys are so shamelessly honest. I do see what you mean about performance-based relationships. A lot of people will not allow themselves to see God as not requiring any service out of us. They think if we see Him as just wanting our presence, we go into the whole 'I don't deserve it mode'. If we are not required to perform, then we could just sit on our spiritual couch and eat spiritual potato chips and get spiritually fat. But when my grandpa was at the end of his life, he didn't desire anything of me other than for me to be with him to keep him company. The result was that I basically gave up everything at that moment to be with him and serve him. Why? Simply because of his unconditional love for me. My uncle couldn't do enough for him. That was his response to his dad's love."

"You're right, Derek. If we allow ourselves to BE who God wants us to be, our hearts will be filled with love, and we will understand the love of God. The result will be heart-born service. Instead, we are taught to have a performance-based relationship with God. In order for us to 'win' His love and approval, we must first serve him. Then He will love us and we will get our spiritual brownie points. That is work done in righteousness (Titus 3:5). Jesus died so we might BECOME the righteousness of God. It is a free gift (Romans 5:17) for us to receive. Once we receive it, we will automatically DO (serve) out of our love for

Him. If someone in the body of Christ is not serving, it is not up to us to 'encourage' him to serve (by telling him to get off his duff and do something). It is our duty to look deeper and to help him find out what is amiss in his heart. Once he becomes healed in his heart, he will serve. I personally think the Church is getting it backwards."

"How did you come to know all this information about the heart? asked Jannie. "You've never said any of this before."

"I didn't have an opportunity until now. Besides, it's not like I had all this wisdom from day one. I had to try things and fail and analyze and try again. If you really want to find out the answer to something, you will eventually."

"I still think Dad would make a good preacher." Ed stood up and walked to the kitchen.

"Yeah, but his sermons would probably be lost on you!" Jannie called after him.

"You're probably right, Jannie," remarked Dad with a tone of resolve in his voice.

If someone in the body of Christ is not serving, it is not up to us to 'encourage' him to serve. It is our duty to look deeper and to help him find out what is amiss in his heart.

"Well, Dad, I may not be that old, but—"

"Hey, who are you calling old?" Dad interrupted.

"Okay, let me rephrase that. I may not be that mature or wise, but I seem to have figured something out," asserted Jannie.

"What's that, sweetheart?" Dad was now much more attentive to Jannie.

"It seems you can approach people with really good information—maybe even good advice that will help them. But unless they are at the point where they are open to receive it, you might as well talk to the cat."

"Unfortunately, you are right. It's like telling a bully to stop bullying. You can't just walk up to a kid and say, 'hey stop bullying me' and expect him to say, 'Oh, sorry, I didn't realize that's what I was doing. I'm going to stop now'."

A long pause lingered while they studied each other's faces as if they held a secret they silently vowed not to share.

"Sorry, Dad, I don't mean to make light of the subject, but that is a ridiculous scenario," Jannie chuckled.

"I know. Bullying is very serious—to the point of people taking their own lives. I just believe we are going about it the wrong way. Instead of making people aware of bullying, shouldn't we be getting therapy for those doing the bullying in order for them to stop? Anyway, that is a whole different topic."

Dad studied his empty glass. "I just hope when Ed finds himself in a relationship and begins to think about racking up points, he remembers what I said. He might still have to make a few mistakes before he fully gets it but, hopefully, it won't turn into a lifetime of failures before it sinks in."

"Okay, Dad, so if you were to give me one piece of advice about my future, what would it be?" asked Jannie.

"Follow your heart. If you look deeply enough, your instinct will tell you what is right. When it does, act on it. There might be a bit of merit to weighing out pros and cons, but in the end, it is just employing logic. Go with what you sense in your heart. That's the best advice I can come up with."

"I do believe it was Eleanor Roosevelt who said, Do what you feel in your heart to be right—for you'll be criticized anyway," said Mom as she snuggled into the chair beside Dad. Princess Diana once said, "Only do what your heart tells you." Mom looked at Dad with sparkling eyes. "It works for me," she grinned.

A long pause lingered while they studied each other's faces as if they held a secret they silently vowed not to share.

Dad broke the silence. "I'll have my pie, now."

CHAPTER 6

"I GET A KICK OUT OF THE WAY YOUR FAMILY interacts together. One minute the conversation is as serious as a high stakes poker game, and the next minute someone is cracking a joke. And it keeps going back and forth," said Derek. He had pulled his car up to the curb in front of Mr. Sherman's house to let Jannie out.

"I guess that is the only way we know how to deal with big issues. Otherwise, they can get rather depressing. Anyway, thanks for the ride, Derek. I will see you later this week."

Derek and Jannie had begun to spend a lot more time together lately. It might have been initiated by the reappearance of Ed in everyone's life, but it may have happened regardless.

Mr. Sherman greeted her at the door. "I have been looking forward to our afternoon tea. I find our visits very refreshing. Ms. Brookes has gone into town to do some errands, but she left tea for us."

Of course she did, thought Jannie. She had never known Ms. Brookes to leave anything undone. She was as efficient as anyone could be and still be human. Jannie had secretly thought something was wrong with her. She was just a little too perfect.

"Come this way," Mr. Sherman jolted her back into reality.

"Does Ms. Brookes have a first name?" It was a rather odd question, but Jannie had said it before she realized it was out.

"Why, of course she does. But from where I come, a title followed by a surname is much more appropriate. I suppose it is only a cultural element, but it has become more of a habit. I expect it does not fit in with our present day lifestyle at all, but after more than 80 years—"

"Yes, I guess that habit would be hard to break."

"So tell me, where are you in your decision making? Have you decided to continue your studies next semester?"

"I wish I could tell you a definite answer, but I do not have one yet. My dad said an interesting thing at dinner the other night. He told me the best advice he could offer was to tell me to follow my heart. I truly believe he is correct. I just don't know how to access that part of me at this point. I don't want to make any mistakes."

> "Does Ms. Brookes have a first name?" It was a rather odd question, but Jannie had said it before she realized it was out.

"I believe your dad is right. You need to learn to live out of your heart. This will help you discover the gifts and callings within you. Then when you have the confidence that you know what you are supposed to do, you will be able to accomplish anything you set out to do. A lot of the time, we know what we are called to do. That's not the issue. Often, the struggle is we listen to so many outside influences. It is quite obvious with artists, musicians and writers. They are the ones who face the greatest obstacles. They are told they cannot make a living in the arts, so they choose professions that are not suited to them just to pay the bills. All the while, the gifts lay dormant—sometimes for a lifetime. Let me read you something."

Mr. Sherman made his way to the nearby bookshelves and surveyed a few books before pulling one out. "Here it is."

"This book by Steven Pressfield is called *The War of Art*. He says, and I quote, 'Creative work is not a selfish act... It's a gift to the world... Don't cheat us of your contribution'.

Parents need to recognize the giftings in their children and steer them in that direction.

"We need to discover your unique calling in life and help you move toward fulfilling it. Only then will you be satisfied—when you have given your contribution to the world.

"In the *International Standard Version of the Bible*, Romans 11:29 states, 'For God's gifts and calling never change'. So, in essence, what He called you to do when you were 11 years old is the same when you are 53. The calling doesn't change. We may take detours and rabbit trails, but that has nothing to do with our original lifework," concluded Mr. Sherman.

"Derek and I touched on this subject several months ago, but I never really pursued answers. In fact, this is probably the reason I was led to talk to you because he felt you would have the insight I needed. So where do I start?"

"It is as your dad said; it is resident in your heart. I think we all know what our calling is, but lots of times, we let so many outside voices dictate to us that we lose sight of what has been inside us all along. For instance, if asked why you live in a certain city or a certain country or why you work at a certain job, you should have one answer only—It's where I'm called. Anything other than that would be a wrong answer. I'm not saying everyone is in their wrong calling. There are definitely those who don't recognize their calling as such but live it out anyway. It just may be they were led by intuition or instinct, a feeling of peace or even the fulfillment of a desire.

"Nevertheless, they fulfilled their calling. Sadly, too many people make career and lifestyle decisions based on everything but their calling. Parents need to recognize the giftings in their children and steer them in that direction. Often, though, parents project their own inadequacies on their children and try to force them to live out an unfulfilled dream from their past."

"I've seen that happen first hand," said Jannie. "I had a girlfriend in school whose mom wanted to be a figure skater, but she injured herself, so she couldn't go on to become a professional. Her daughter, on the other hand, was into everything related to science. But instead of nurturing her interests, her mother drove her to the skating rink every morning before school to practice. I always felt sorry for for my friend."

"So what became of her?" asked Mr. Sherman.

"She is at a university studying astronomy. She probably never again went near a skating rink after she left home."

"I'm sure some tension lingers in the family still because of it," interjected Mr. Sherman. "Sad. I think children should be allowed to explore and flourish in the area they are called. It's heartbreaking to see kids be manipulated into someone else's agenda for their lives. As for your own life, it's not too late. You're young. Go only where you are called. Go only if your heart leads you. If you go for any other reason, it's the wrong one."

It's heartbreaking to see kids be manipulated into someone else's agenda for their lives.

Jannie smiled affectionately at Mr. Sherman. "Everyone should have a mentor like you."

"Haha, not everyone wants one or even realizes they should be mentored."

"I best be going," she said. "I have a few errands to tend to before I go home today."

"It's been a pleasurable afternoon, young lady."

CHAPTER 7

J ANNIE STUMBLED OVER THE CURB AND ONTO THE sidewalk. She managed not to fall, but her handbag was not so fortunate. Bang. Down it went dumping half its contents on the cement walk. She managed to gather up the scattered items quickly and grabbed her cell phone to see if it still worked. There was a missed message from Victoria, a lady she had met at college. Odd that she would be messaging her. They hadn't seen each other in several months, but when they did get together last, she and Victoria had clicked. Jannie messaged back with arrangements to meet later in the week. She scurried off to her appointment. Shoot. Now for sure she was going to be late!

The first few minutes with Victoria brought emotions rushing back to Jannie. She felt the same way she did when she was in college. This made her realize how much had changed since she decided to take a break.

Victoria had soft brown hair and inviting eyes that danced when she talked. Her nails were perfectly manicured as if she had just been to a salon. She didn't fit Jannie's image of a lawyer at all. Victoria was older than Jannie. She arrived as a mature student looking to get a law degree. She was able to skip the first four years because of qualifying life experiences. She wasn't old enough to be Jannie's mother, but she was not in her peer group either. From what Jannie remembered, Victoria had struggled with a relationship she was committed to but had reservations about. She leaned forward on the table as if to reveal some hidden secret.

"I'm at a crossroads, Jannie, and I need someone who is well removed from the situation to help me see clearly. I thought about some of our conversations and, well, I kept picturing more of the same."

"What seems to be your biggest dilemma?" asked Jannie.

I was never treated that way when I was growing up, so it's very archaic to me. It's as if I were a woman stuck in the 1950s.

"I didn't notice it at first. You know, the initial stages of romance and the newness of a relationship tend to mask a lot of underlying issues. However, a recurring subtle theme did crop up, which I can't seem to shake. He says he respects my choice to pursue a law degree and eventually a practice, but he portrays an underlying jealousy, and I think he's subconsciously trying to sabotage my career."

"Wow, are you sure that's what it is?" Jannie had little experience in this arena. She was feeling out of her comfort zone. Nevertheless, she wanted to be there for Victoria.

"It's odd that I didn't notice it before, but he makes a lot of gender stereotypical comments. I was never treated that way when I was growing up, so it's very archaic to me. It's as if I were a woman stuck in the 1950s trying to break out of the classic housewife mould. Or worse yet, like I'm living in the early 1900s before women were allowed to vote."

Victoria laughed at her own statement as if it were absurd. Jannie smiled, relieved for a break in the intensity of the conversation.

Victoria abruptly changed the subject.

"Wow, time has gone by so fast, and I must run to my next class. I hope I didn't come across too heavy for you, Jannie. I just needed a listening ear. I don't expect you to solve my problems for me, but if you have any input, I'd greatly appreciate."

"You know, Victoria, I don't at the moment. But I do promise to find out something for you."

After Victoria left, Jannie made her way to the bus stop outside the College campus grounds and sat on a nearby bench. She opened her tablet while she waited for the next bus. A few key words from Victoria's conversation stuck out, so she typed them into the search engine. She came across a video of a speaker she had heard a few times before—this would pass the time while she rode the bus across the city. She hit the play button.

"Gender stereotypes," the speaker began. "We hear it all the time. 'Oh, it's a guy thing' or 'I just can't understand women'."

The speaker was anything but stereotypical. Her casual shirt and jeans added to the androgynous look that she was subtly portraying.

"Beyond the obvious physical differences, it's true we are different in the way our minds work and we differ psychologically. BUT, when we take into consideration only the sensical, physical realm, we dismiss the most vital component of our make up—our spirit. Essentially, we are spirit beings housed in a physical body. The body is operated by a mind that reasons, a will that allows us freedom of choice, and emotions with which to feel. If we continue to operate solely on the levels of the physical, mental and emotional, we will never understand or get along with the opposite sex. The chasm between genders will simply be driven wider.

"So why were we created male and female? So we could spend a lifetime in conflict and in the end be resolved that the person we married was the wrong one? Is it just to have children so the human race can be preserved while generation after generation can continue to live in strife and conflict with the opposing gender? I believe marriage was designed to bring together two halves of a whole. Where one partner is missing a component, the other can provide it. Where did we get the idea that in order to be compatible, we have to be just like our partner with similar interests and preferences? Why should a husband be disappointed when his wife doesn't want to go on a fishing trip? Why would a woman demand that her husband be dragged through a mall for hours on end? I chuckle that I've used stereotypes to illustrate my point, but I think you get my drift.

"If truth be told, I'm the one who visits a mall on only 2–3 occasions a year while my husband goes grocery shopping almost every day. But back to the original reason for which marriage was designed. I truly believe men and women are capable of meeting each other's needs, especially emotionally. Where we have gone wrong is in generations of hurt little boys raising sons without recognizing their owns hurts and not allowing for healing to take place. Or many children are being brought up in single parent situations in which one partner is absent. Often these children are at a disadvantage because they don't learn to relate to the parent who is missing. Through generations of unhealed hearts, we have perpetuated the myth that opposing genders can't coexist without strife and conflict, thereby continuing the cycle."

Jannie paused the video for a moment so she could absorb what she had just heard. She looked around the bus—nothing unusually interesting. Most of the people had exited the bus, leaving her almost alone. She straightened her headphones and resumed the video.

"We continue to stereotype people because of gender instead of allowing people to be individuals. God created us each to be individuals and I for one have grown weary of being labelled as odd because I like to collect cars. I mean real ones that take up garage space, not the ones from the toy store that gather dust on family room shelves. I'm actually more passionate about cars than my mechanic husband. I still confront many egos when I arrive in my own separate vehicle at car shows." The speaker paused and rolled her eyes.

Where we have gone wrong is in generations of hurt little boys raising sons without recognizing their owns hurts and not allowing for healing to take place.

"When we treat each person as an individual regardless of gender, we go to a higher level and are able to communicate with that person on a spirit (heart) level. When we begin to get in the habit of operating from our hearts rather than just the 'sense' realm, the stereotypes begin to fade.

"As for being compatible, I've heard it said that when you search for a spouse, you should find someone with whom you are compatible. I think, however, it's not much of a compatibility issue than an availability or accessibility issue. If your heart is sealed off and you become emotionally unavailable or you just don't function from the heart, you will have conflict. No amount of compatibility can compensate for a closed heart."

The bus abruptly screeched to a stop. Startled, Jannie quickly gathered her belongings and got off the bus. The short walk to her house was refreshing in the fall air, the trees turning amber and light brown hues.

The next morning, Jannie awoke with Victoria's situation still at the forefront of her mind. She knew Victoria's revelation would continue to plague her mind until she had another conversation with her. Did she not have enough to think about without taking on someone else's problems? I guess not. This was a part of Jannie's personality that really bugged her. She decided to contact Mr. Sherman. It was not a day they usually got together, but she went over anyway.

You've heard that actions speak louder than words. Well, when the two are in conflict, we tend to believe the actions.

"What seems to be on your mind?" asked Mr. Sherman in a light tone. He always seemed ready to help solve any perplexity.

"May I ask your advice for a friend of mine? Since you have a lot of insight into heart matters, I am sure you can shed some light on the situation."

"A real friend or a fictional one?"

"Oh, haha, no. I mean a real friend. Her name is Victoria. I met her at the college, and she called me the other day wanting my input on her relationship." Jannie proceeded to recount to Mr. Sherman the details Victoria had shared with her.

"You know, it's not so much about the circumstances or situations. I believe it is more about the message this man is conveying to her by his actions. You've heard that actions speak louder than words. Well, when the two are in conflict, we tend to believe the actions. What is he telling her subliminally?

"Messages received become beliefs that reside in the heart. Messages are imparted to us by others through their words and actions toward us. They usually do not come in the form of a 'talk' in which someone sits you down and says, 'I'd like to tell you about this...' Most often they come when we least expect them. Messages can be communicated through a glance, either with approval or disapproval. They come through a comment, either derogatory or edifying. Often they are not specifically directed at us. However, dependent upon the condition of our own hearts, the words or actions might be interpreted in a way the speaker never intended. They can be perceived as meaning something they weren't meant to convey.

"However, that doesn't change the fact that a message has been received. The strength of that message depends on the faith or trust we have in the person imparting it. The power behind the message is dependent on the amount of influence that person has in our life. I have met people who I would trust with my life. On the other hand, I know people I don't have the faith in to get me across the room. They are people I've observed over time and found to be all talk and no action or people who pretend to have my best interest at heart but instead simply have their own agenda to put forth."

"That reminds me, have you ever noticed people who," asked Jannie, "when you begin speaking about a situation or problem in your life interrupt before you finish? Instead of listening intently, they immediately jump in with their advice on how to fix a situation. It seems they are satisfying the fact they know something and want to hear themselves speak rather than genuinely wanting to help you."

"That's when you know they have unresolved heart issues and probably need more help than you do," said Mr. Sherman. "You have a choice to receive a message in your heart or not. Especially if it makes you feel unworthy, you need to assess the amount of influence you think this person should have on your life. If you decide they are not in a position to properly communicate a message to your heart, then take their information with a grain of salt.

"When messages are received, whether good or bad, they become part of our inner programming. Dr. Jerry Savelle said, 'When we were born, we were not born to be losers. The trouble is we've allowed other people to program us to fail'.

"Where does programming reside? In the heart. Sure, it comes into us through what we observe or what we listen to, where we form thoughts. Those thoughts that we entertain become beliefs that form the basis of our programming.

"And whatever our programming is, it stays in our heart until either we allow ourselves to be reprogrammed or we die. Until then, a person will never rise above what he or she believes. If you have an inherent belief you are ugly, no amount of fancy clothing, make-up, weight loss, or plastic surgery will change that belief. You just can't change the outside, expecting to change the inside because it all comes from within. To experience a change, first the heart needs reconfiguration. Behavioural patterns stem from reactions to beliefs formed from information that was deposited in the heart. Often, the information is wrong and the belief is taken from misconstrued messages.

"Here's am example of what I am talking about. I knew of a married couple. The husband constantly refered to their possessions in the singular possessive—'my house', 'my bed', 'my yard', etc. He never realized the subliminal message he was sending to his wife. She, however, never felt she could come up to the level of equal partner because of his actions. In her heart, she did not feel welcomed into his life or comfortable in 'his surroundings' simply because of the way he conveyed things to her or to other people. The husband didn't realize he was pushing her away. After a while, he got frustrated at his lack of enthusiasm for their marriage. When confronted, he would say they were equal, but the pattern never changed."

"So what is the solution? asked Jannie. "I guess if you don't like the results, you should change your method of communication. Figure out which messages you are sending through your actions and then do the opposite? As you mentioned earlier, we've all heard that actions speak louder than words. I didn't realize, though, that whenever the two are in conflict, the other person will believe your actions instead of your words. So if you want to change the message, you need to change the method of delivery. Right?"

"Well, yes, in theory," agreed Mr. Sherman. "The trouble is, if you only change your actions, that simply becomes behaviour modification. Trying to change your behaviour without changing the root of the action can work only for a while. Unfortunately, when a stressful situation arises, we default back to previous behaviour.

"Let me tell you what I have observed about patterns—patterns of behaviour. Many life coaches talk about habits. To me, patterns are slightly different because we are able to develop or change habits from the outside, meaning behaviour modification. I tend to notice patterns. It's like the rule of cause and effect—but with a deeper root. For example, I worked with a lady whom I would call intense. She wanted to do a lot of things and liked to reach out and help a lot of people, but she would get

> Behavioural patterns stem from reactions to beliefs formed from information that was deposited in the heart.

sucked into 'beyond normal' levels of stress. The closer an event she was planning got, the more angry she became. She would blame this or that person, or she became angry that a certain situation wasn't going the way she thought it should go or would have liked it to go. She treated each incident as isolated and as if had only this or that been different, everything would have been perfect. After a while, I began to see patterns in her behaviour, and I realized it wasn't the actual circumstances causing the stress but simply the triggering of a pattern of behaviour on which she was accustomed to acting out. It got to the point where I removed myself emotionally from the events in order to keep my sense of peace as best as I could.

"We can draw attention to destructive patterns in the hopes that the realization will cause change in another, but usually the change comes from behaviour modification that can last only as long as the person's will power. Pattern changes can be altered only from within us by changing the beliefs in our hearts. You can't change the fruit until you change the root, remember?"

Pattern changes can be altered only from within us by changing the beliefs in our hearts.

"How could I forget?" Jannie smiled. With that remark, she closed her laptop and returned it to her bag. "I really think I need to talk to Victoria. I want to relay this to her while it is fresh in my mind. I am sure all this will be revelation to her, and it just may help her make the decision she's been looking to make. Do you mind if we continue this another day?"

"Not at all. I am not going anywhere," concluded Mr. Sherman.

Jannie made her way to the car, thinking of everything Mr. Sherman had said, trying to put the conversation into her own words to relay to her friend. A few minutes later, she was turning onto the familiar street of her neighborhood. She swung the car into the driveway, parked and pulled out her phone.

"Hi, Victoria?" Jannie started. "Do you have a minute?"

"Sure," came the response from the other end of her cellphone. "What's up?"

"I might have a bit of revelation for you. I know I didn't have any answers or insight the other day when we talked, but I've been thinking about ever since."

"Oh, good," Victoria's voice was fading."I hoped you would be able to see something that I couldn't."

"I'm not sure if this will help or not, but I think this whole distinction between genders is probably just a symptom of something bigger at a subliminal level. I honestly believe a much deeper-rooted problem exists with this guy, and you are seeing only the evidence on the surface. Not sure if this is helpful or not, but I wanted to share it with you anyway."

"Let me think about it for a bit and maybe we can get together in a day or two. I am studying for an exam right now, so I am a bit distracted."

"Yeah, we'll talk soon."

Jannie hung up the phone and ascended the walk to her parent's front door. It was time to relax and shut out the rest of the world for now.

CHAPTER 8

MR. SHERMAN SEEMED UNUSUALLY CHIPPER today. Not that he was any less bubbly on other days. Today, though, he had an added sparkle to him. When Jannie walked into his home, she expected they would meet in the library as they often did. She loved the atmosphere of being surrounded by all those books—so much knowledge, so much wisdom. She felt she could conquer anything she needed to by simply opening one of those magic-filled pages and beginning to read. She followed Mr. Sherman down the hallway that led to the library.

"I would like to show you something," he said.

They stopped short of entering the double doors to the library. To the right was a room concealed by a wood-framed glass door with several individual panes. The door was covered from behind by a heavy curtain that completely blocked the view of the inside of the room. Jannie had walked past the door several times when entering the library. She just assumed it was a guest bedroom.

"Go ahead," Mr. Sherman stood to the side and turned the door-knob only enough to unlatch it from the frame. Jannie moved ahead and pushed open the door. The room was a lot cooler than the rest of the house, but she quickly forgot about the temperature when she laid eyes on the focal piece of furniture. A baby grand piano sat angled in the far corner of the room opposite the door. A small octagonal window was set above and to the right, which caught the afternoon light and backlit the soundboard accenting the exposed strings. The housing lid was open and propped at an angle to provide a louder, more resonant sound. The piano was as long as it was wide, creating an almost perfect square.

"Wow, I don't think I've ever seen a white grand piano."

"It's Ivory coloured actually. They are quite rare.

"Isabella wanted a grand her whole life, so when she turned 50, it seemed like the right time. She would play it for hours on end. She never tired of it."

"What sort of music did she play?"

"She was classically trained, so she played a lot of the masters. Sometimes, I think, she wanted to see how fast her fingers could go up and down the keyboard; the music she made was simply a bonus."

Jannie studied the sturdy square legs that tapered off and then abruptly turned into large blocks at the bottom. The clean straight lines and glossy finish contradicted the style of furniture in the rest of the house that was dark-coloured wood pieces classified as Queen Anne or Louis XVI. The room was obviously designated to the fine instrument, which was encircled by two curvilinear settees facing the keyboard.

As if to read Jannie's mind, Mr. Sherman continued his discourse. "It was not the style Isabella would have chosen at first. I think she would have wanted a much more ornate piece of furniture with a cherry finish. That would, however, mean we would be looking for a piano close to 100 years old. That is about the lifespan of these beauties. In order to get a desired sound quality, all the inner working parts would have had to be replaced. A lot of time and money would be consumed before the instrument reached a level of quality of today's new instruments—not to mention how difficult it would be to find someone qualified to do the work. Ultimately, it was the feel and sound of this piano that won her over. The gentleman in the piano store looked at me and said, 'this is definitely your wife's piano'. And it was. I long for the day she returns and serenades me once again with her lovely melodies. She may not have been the most talented pianist, but her heart was definitely in it.

> We would be looking for a piano close to 100 years old. That is about the lifespan of these beauties.

"Would you like to try it?"

"Oh, no," Jannie gasped in surprise. "I couldn't, really."

"Go ahead. I am sure Isabella would be pleased."

Jannie felt as if she had forgotten every note she had ever learned in lessons as a child. Playing an instrument was not something she had desired. It was her mother who insisted she try until she gave up in exasperation as Jannie refused to practice day after day. It did not take long for the family to discover that playing the piano was not her favourite pastime. Jannie looked at Mr. Sherman's face and thought she dare not disappoint him, so she sat on the leather seat of the bench. Slowly she raised her hands to the keys and began to plunk out a lullaby her mother had taught her early on.

"Wow, that truly is a stunning sound." remarked Jannie.

"It is very captivating." Mr. Sherman smiled. "I miss hearing it every day."

Jannie heard a shuffle and turned around to see Ms. Brookes whisk past with a tray. She stopped abruptly before the library door. She appeared startled as if she were not expecting to see anyone in the music room.

"Tea is ready," she called and then disappeared.

In the library, Jannie and Mr. Sherman took their respective places.

"Mr. Sherman," Jannie began. "If you were to sum up what you want me to learn from you in one sentence, what would it be?"

"That is a tall order, my dear. But I do believe I have one key point I would like to impart. It's all about the heart. Everything we do, everything we say, everything we believe or don't believe, everything we are—all stem from what is within our heart. I think you phrased it well when you said we need to stop trying to change the fruit and look for the source of issues at the root. The root is the heart."

Mr. Sherman made his way over to his desk against the far wall. He opened the long drawer in the middle and pulled out a large black book before seating himself again.

"And this is what I have learned over the last many decades about the heart."

He opened the book and thumbed through the first few pages. It was a leather-bound notebook with decades' worth of worn pages. From what she could see, Jannie assumed this had been compiled over a lifetime.

"May I take notes?" asked Jannie.

"Please do. I have a lot of them myself, so we may not get through this in a single session." Jannie reached into her bag and extracted her laptop.

"If I were to sum up what I want you to learn from me in one sentence, what would it be? This is one of the first questions I began asking about life—why do people do what they do? And I would have to say, it is all a reflection of what is in our hearts.

"If there was one thing only that I could stress to you, it is to do as Proverbs 4:23 says: 'Guard your heart WITH ALL DILI-GENCE for out of it flows the issues of life'. That says to me that the heart is the most essential part of the being, and it should be protected at all costs. Another translation says 'Above all else, guard your heart. The heart is a very precious commodity, Jan-nie. We must keep it clear of all negative facets. If we don't guard our hearts with all diligence, out of it will flow the WRONG is-sues of life. Not that we can stop all offences or hurts that come our way, but we can certainly choose whether or not to allow them to stay. If we nurse or rehearse hurtful circumstances, we nurture the offence and allow it to take root in our heart."

"But how do you avoid that?" Jannie asked with slight frustra-tion evidenced in her tone. "There is so much negativity coming at us every day; it is difficult to remain in a healthy state all the time."

"You're right. Offences and hurts will come, but if you become quick to eliminate them, they won't stay or take root in your heart."

"But how do you do that? It seems difficult," asked Jannie.

"The first step in getting one's heart healed is to forgive. Having said that, I know much misconception abounds around the meaning of forgiveness. First of all, it does not condone the action of the person who offended or caused hurt. In fact, it really has nothing further to do with the action of the offender. As I told my sons when they were young—be selfish. Forgive. I added that bit of shock value in order to make them think and also so they remembered it more easily. By being selfish, I meant you are doing yourself a favor by forgiving the actions of others, even if they don't ask for forgiveness, even if they don't acknowledge any wrongdoing. The idea is to put off the feeling of being offended so you yourself don't suffer any consequences from holding a grudge. It doesn't mean you disregard the behaviour of the other person or that you deny an offence ever happened. It also doesn't mean you have to allow that person to remain in your circle of influence. Forgiveness simply means you reject the offence and it no longer has control over you. You see, when Jesus was telling us to to forgive, it wasn't so we could gain God's approval or become martars. It was always for our benefit. He was saying forgive so you can be healthy and whole.

The idea [of forgiveness] is to put off the feeling of being offended so you yourself don't suffer any consequences from holding a grudge.

"Years ago, my wife, Isabella, owned a business. After running it for a few years, she realized she didn't like being the boss, so she listed it for sale with a real estate company. The trouble was it wasn't selling as quickly as she liked. When an acquaintance of hers offered to run it for her while she took a less stressful job, she took her associate up on the offer. It was not long before she discovered that the acquaintance was running her business down by funnelling Isabella's customers into a new business. Isabella came to me in tears one night, almost at a crisis point. She could look the other way and hoped the business sold quickly before there was nothing left, or she could try to figure out how to deal with the situation.

The words simple and easy are used synonymously, but they are not synonyms. In this case, the solution was simple but it WAS one of the hardest things she had done.

"I asked Isabella, 'What is the hardest thing you could do right now?'

"After several minutes of thought, she answered that the most difficult thing would be to take back management of her business while still working full time. By simply acknowledging that fact seemed to give her a glimmer of hope. Once that hope was born on her heart, she took the steps to make it happen. Was it difficult? Absolutely. Many times, we make things a lot more complicated than they really are. Even though things may be simple to change, they may not be easy. That is the problem. Often, solutions are close at hand, but they may be difficult and that is why we do not solve issues. The words *simple* and *easy* are used synonymously, but they are not synonyms. In this case, the solution was simple but it WAS one of the hardest things she had done.

"Isabella wanted the 'yucky' feeling to go away, and she sensed the only way out was to let her acquaintance go and once again take over management of the business herself. She knew it would be a short-term situation. And it was. As soon as she made the decision to do it, the energy came from within and people rallied with her to help. Later, after the business was sold, she seemed relieved. But when the dust finally settled, she still had an unresolved feeling in her heart.

"On examination, she found that even though the circumstances had changed, something was still amiss. She had not actually forgiven her acquaintance. She needed to forgive the lady for her own sake in order to get peace. She examined her heart and realized she had sensed from the start not to let the lady take over the business. Isabella took ownership of the fact she went against her heart and took the easy way out. Ultimately, it ended up being the hard way out. Isabella didn't place blame, though. Instead, she took full responsibility for the situation, knowing she could have avoided it if she had listened to and followed her heart in the first place. Over the next few days, she wrote a seven-page letter to the lady outlining how she felt and how she perceived what happened. Once the letter was sent, Isabella felt free. It never bothered her again, and whenever she spoke of it—other than to use the situation as an example—it was to help someone else.

"So healing begins with forgiveness and according to Matthew 18:35, it is done at a heart level. '... If each of you does not forgive his brother FROM HIS HEART!' (HCSB) Isabella forgave her, but I also must stress they didn't remain close friends. Isabella's forgiveness of her didn't do anything to change the other woman, so to let her remain in Isabella's life would be to allow her to continue to cause hurt. You need to forgive, but you don't need to be stupid.

"It's much like bullying."

"Oh, yeah," Jannie interjected, "My dad brought that subject up the other day, too. It's been talked about a lot lately. People are trying to create awareness of bullying so it will stop."

"That's commendable. We all want bullying to stop. However, I don't think just drawing attention to it will actually cause it to stop. In my opinion, you can't just approach people and tell them their actions are that of a bully and they need to stop."

"That's almost exactly what my dad said!"

"He's a very smart man. When you say things like that, you are not really empowering the person to stop. If anything, the warning could trigger more anger with more negative results. Bullying, I believe, stems from an unresolved hurt in the heart. Bullies probably have no idea why they do what they do, or how to stop it."

"So how does one get it to stop?"

"Well, it goes back to what we discussed earlier," said Mr. Sherman. "We tend to treat symptoms instead of curing the ill at the root. In my opinion, we should spend less time drawing attention to the fruit—bullying—and start focusing on the root—unresolved issues of the heart. If we cure the root, we will change—or in this case eliminate—the bad fruit.

"My advice to a victim of bullying is first to tell someone. We usually can't fight these things on our own, so get help. Having allies, especially strong ones, does two things. First, it helps the victim bolster his or her confidence and not feel so helpless. Second, it makes a statement to bullies that they are not just fighting a single weak entity.

"Another thing is not to allow fear to take hold. I am not saying to deny fear. It is a very real force, but if you make the decision not to let it grip you, that alone begins to empower you to change your situation.

"Another tactic is to stop dwelling on the act of bullying and begin to look behind it. Ask yourself why is that person doing this?

What is lacking in that person or what circumstance caused him or her to do this? Start to see the bully in a different light. Start to view the bully as the victim who is simply acting out instead of seeing yourself as the victim. This will enable you to more freely forgive the bully. Sometimes, showing bullies compassion will disarm them.

"Have you ever heard the story of the Cross and the Switch-blade?"

"No, I haven't," Jannie answered.

"It's the true life story of evangelist David Wilkerson's encounter with gang leader Nicky Cruz back in the 1960s. Cruz threatened to kill Wilkerson, but Wilkerson stood up to him and told him instead that Jesus loved him. Cruz later surrendered his life to Jesus because of Wilkerson's boldness. That to me is the ultimate bullying story. And I am not saying everyone should do the same. Each situation is unique. In fact, my advice is to remove yourself from the situation as best and as quickly as you can, no matter how that has to be done. Forgive the person and then get away. But always stay in close contact with your allies. Call them at all times when you are feeling powerless. Get them to help you in whatever way they can."

We can't talk about the heart without talking about love. I mean real love, the kind in which you would give your life for another person.

"Could it be that bullying is a form of overcompensating for an inadequacy in the bully's life?" Jannie asked.

"Usually, it is the absence of love. We can't talk about the heart without talking about love. I mean real love, the kind in which you would give your life for another person. You can see the evidence of love every time you see giving because that is what love does; it gives. When you bully someone, you are taking something away from that person. Bullying is robbing others of their self-worth. Most likely, bullies do not feel in control of their own feelings or circumstances, so attempting to take control of someone else's life can give them a feeling of power.

"On a lesser scale, I have seen people who have a need to be in control of everything under the guise of helping. They think they are helping others, but they often overstep boundaries and begin to take control. Again, it is done at a subconscious level, which is probably why they get so hurt when the people they are 'helping' reject their input. Excuse me for using derogatory labels, but I refer to this kind of person as a control freak."

When others still won't conform, control freaks push them out of their lives. That's when they launch into victim mode and blame the other person for the outcome.

Jannie laughed. She was a bit shocked at Mr. Sherman's comment. It seemed so out of character for him to say something so boldly informal.

"I actually feel sorry for control freaks. When they don't get the outcome they want, they have to live in the toxicity of offence. If you watch people who try to control everything, you will see a pattern: Control, Offence, and Victim. They try to control others, but when the outcome is not what they desired, they become offended at them. Once offended, they will use emotion like anger as manipulation. When others still won't conform, control freaks push them out of their lives. That's when they launch into victim mode and blame the other person for the outcome. This is an example of a friendship that is dependent on others' fulfill-ment of their expectations."

"Performance-based relationships!" exclaimed Jannie.

"Yes, I guess you can call them that," replied Mr. Sherman, a little surprised.

"I see it now. My dad was talking to Ed and Derek about perfor-mance-based relationships. The reason they are so dysfunctional is because they are a form of control. If you do what I want, you get rewarded, if you don't, then you get punished. It's like train-ing a dog. Hopefully, most of us have elevated to a level above the canine species."

"I don't think we take the subject of control seriously enough," stated Mr. Sherman. Most of the time, it is a very evil force. On the topic of control, you've probably heard it said, 'God is in control'. A lot of churches perpetuate this belief. Even popu-lar Christian songs have been written about the topic. You've probably also heard the statement 'God is Sovereign'? The Bible actually says the opposite. First of all, in Genesis 1:26, God says He gave us dominion over His creation. The dictionary defines *dominion* as 'sovereign as authority'. Well, if He gave the author-ity to us, then it stands to reason He doesn't have it anymore. Also, in Psalm 115:16, He says, 'The heavens are the heavens of the LORD, But the earth He has given to the sons of men' (NASB). Sure, He has all the power in the universe—and the ability to do astronomically what we couldn't even imagine, but He gave up authority by His own choice. He limited His own power when He gave it to us. The age-old question is, 'If God is in control, why are so many people suffering on a daily basis?' My answer is God is not in control.

"It goes back to Love again. God is Love. Love does not con-trol. Love does not destroy. Love does not cause hurt on a daily basis. Love values, regards highly, and holds people special. Fear controls. I believe those who are in the greatest amount of fear exercise the greatest amount of control. Control, in its extreme, is the spirit of murder."

"What?" asked Jannie.

"It makes sense, doesn't it? Murder is taking control over someone and robbing that person of life. It is committing an act against the will of another. It removes someone's ability to choose for himself or herself. Think about it. Evil is not just an act. Evil resides in the heart. Take the case of Judas. That wasn't just a random, misguided act that caused him to betray the Lord Jesus Christ. No, his heart was full of evil. He was the treasurer of the 'Jesus of Nazareth's Evangelical Ministry', but he was stealing from the coffers. The Bible states in 1 Timothy 6:10: 'The LOVE of money is the root of all evil'. Notice this verse does not say money is the root of all evil. Money is simply a vehicle by which we can trade goods and services. Money in itself is neither good nor evil. But the LOVE of money is the root of ALL evil. Where does love reside? In the heart. Had Judas' heart been filled with other things, the outcome would have been entirely different— because of his occupation, one would assume Judas' heart would be filled with the love of God. I believe God knew his heart all along and used him to fulfil the plan of the ultimate sacrifice."

Jannie closed her laptop as if to say she was done. She stared at the wall of books beside her. What Mr. Sherman was telling her was far beyond the scope of her small world. This information was for more than just her. She must be diligent in recording it because from what she knew at this point, many people out there needed to hear what she was learning.

"Difficult to absorb it all, isn't it? Never mind. Let's leave it at that for today." Mr. Sherman stood up and walked to the window. "I just love the colours of this season. Fall is my favourite time of year."

CHAPTER 9

A FEW DAYS WENT BY SINCE JANNIE'S LAST VISIT TO Mr. Sherman's. Today, Mom lent her the car, and she was able to make more efficient use of her time than when she had to rely on public transit.

She pulled up to a busy intersection just as the light turned red. As she daydreamed, a man pushing a shopping cart crossed in front of her car. By the look of his clothing, hair and the overflow of trash bags in his cart, she concluded he must be a homeless person. Immediately, she felt compassion toward the man. Soon, however, her mind switched from thinking of how she could help him to an overwhelming feeling of guilt over her present circumstances. She had never been without shelter, food or clothing for even a day. Yet, this man probably spent most of his waking hours concerned with getting the necessities to make it through to the next day.

A few minutes later, the incident fresh in her mind, she described the scene to Mr. Sherman.

"I felt guilty that I had to keep going with the traffic and that I could do nothing at the moment to ease his plight."

"I understand the feeling, Jannie, but believe it or not, guilt is not an appropriate response. Guilt is actually disempowering but that's another subject for another day. I used to have guilty feelings regarding homeless people because I had more material goods and a comfortable place to live. But let me tell you a story about what happened to Isabella and I that changed all that.

"One day, a few years ago, a man stumbled into the church we were attending in a downtown district of the city. Our church was smack dab in the middle of what the city deemed the red zone because it was inhabited by street people, drug addicts and prostitutes. The service had ended and the luncheon that had been served afterward was mostly cleaned up and put away. The man was tearful, said he was hungry, so we proceeded to get him a cup of coffee and a sandwich. An addictions counselor, who was part of the congregation, spoke with him as he ate. After a lengthy conversation, the counselor made the assessment that this man was at the end of his rope and wanted out of his present lifestyle. He had nothing but the clothes on his back. My wife and I made the decision to provide him with whatever help we could. While Isabella telephoned contacts to get him into a safehouse for the night, I took him to a nearby department store and outfitted him with new jeans, shoes, socks and a warm coat. We then drove him to the safehouse where he would have up to three nights of free accommodation. As he climbed out of the backseat of our newly purchased car, he commented that he felt like he had just been chauffeured in the back of a limousine.

Word on the street filtered back to us that he had returned to his former lifestyle of drug dealing and addiction.

"We all felt so good about the fact we were able to make a difference in the life of this man. Meanwhile, the addictions counselor worked at finding more permanent accommodations. Once pulled out from his former lifestyle, he would be on his way to making a new life for himself. Right? Sadly, this was not the case. He left the safehouse before his time was up, leaving instructions not to pursue him. Word on the street filtered back to us that he had returned to his former lifestyle of drug dealing and addiction. In his case, all the outward changes did nothing to facilitate an inward change of the heart. I've come to believe the reason people come to live on the streets is less about what they lack in the material realm and more about what they believe about themselves in their hearts.

"Don't get me wrong; I have deep compassion for the predicament of the homeless. Each one is an individual with his or her own story and unique set of circumstances. For a lot of them, though, it is not a lack of worldly goods or opportunities that results in their present condition. For many, their condition can only be addressed and reversed from the inside first. Who you are is a product of what you believe in your heart. Since each of us is ultimately responsible for the condition of our own hearts, we can't force anyone to adopt a new lifestyle. They first must recognize from where this stems and be able to take the steps to change from within."

"So, are you ready to take notes?" Mr. Sherman abruptly switched subjects.

Jannie chuckled, a bit startled at his brusque manner. "I should have been taking notes the first day I met you. I would have had an encyclopedia written by now. Where were you when I was struggling to get my homework done on time?" she teased.

"Well, I have close to six decades of life experience—more than you do, so I hope I know a thing or two."

Jannie stared at the notebook that Mr. Sherman had open on his lap.

"How is it you just happen to have a book filled with notes on the heart, so when I ask questions, you have the answers at your fingertips? This is more than a coincidence."

"I have always been curious. I made myself a student of human nature from an early age. I did not take everything for face value. I studied people and their motives because I was interested not so much in what they were doing but why they were doing it.

"My first recollection of this was when I was still a teenager and left home to find a job. Back then, the most important thing was to earn enough money to eat, but we will save the history lesson for later. I grew up in moderate surroundings—with very little experience of life in the big city, so I tended to be quite trusting of people. It only took a couple of times for that trust to be broken before I learned that not everyone was like me.

"This might sound like I am changing the topic, but bear with me. Proverbs 23:7 is an often quoted verse in Christian circles. The NKJV states, 'For as he thinks in his heart, so is he'. I am sure you have heard that more than once. But the second half of the verse is not as often cited. 'Eat and drink!' He says to you, But his heart is not with you'. This describes the man who does one thing on the outside but has a very different view in his heart.

To me the first part of the verse was out of context, especially when I read the few surrounding verses. The New International Version states, 'Do not eat the food of a begrudging host, do not crave his delicacies; for he is the kind of person who is always thinking about the cost. 'Eat and drink,' He says to you, but his heart is not with you. You will vomit up the little you have eaten and will have wasted your compliments'."

"Which verses are those?" asked Jannie.

"Proverbs 23:6–8. I spent a lot of time observing people and analyzing their actions. This is where I began to see how important it was to have integrity in my own life. I knew I couldn't change the people around me, but I did not have to be like them. And I certainly did not have to allow them to experience my close friendship.

"May I tell you one of my pet peeves? Very few people really bother me. However, if I meet someone who is phony, someone with a false persona, I become really irritated."

"You? I can't imagine you being bugged by anyone," marvelled Jannie.

"No, it's true. If there is one thing I can't stand, it is a fake. You know the type? They have a front to them, and they act as if they are hiding something. Maybe not everyone sees through them like I do, but I find it rather disturbing.

"If you've ever spent any time around me, you will start to notice that I don't like anything that is not real. I won't even allow fake plants in my house because of what they represent. I understand the idea behind the mentality of 'fake it till you make it'. And to a point, I agree with it. I personally believe it should be called 'Faith it until you make it'. That would be a more accurate expression. The idea is to say and act like things have come to pass before they actually have. The reason it works is because the mind will begin to believe what the mouth is saying, and it will subconsciously believe the subsequent actions are reality. Unfortunately, if there is no change at the heart level, the 'fake' becomes the new reality.

> Very few people really bother me. However, if I meet someone who is phony, someone with a false persona, I become really irritated

"Often, people put up a great front when they are around others in order to make themselves look good. As long as they wear the plastic mask, no one can see the hurt that resides in their heart. In fact, they are so skilled at the act that they even fool themselves. But what happens when a crisis hits? Or even when a stressful situation occurs? That is when the logical thought process gets bypassed and the real inner being takes over. One does not have to look very far to see the actions controlled by the inner being—usually the abundance of the heart can be heard quite plainly coming out of the mouth. Who you are when nobody is looking is who you really are.

People put up a great front when they are around others in order to make themselves look good. As long as they wear the plastic mask, no one can see the hurt that resides in their heart.

"A problem arises when the heart is sealed off because of past hurts or offences. That's when the 'fake' becomes the norm, turns into a lifestyle, and lasts a lifetime. The person hiding behind the false front can't see what's happening. Most other people can. Sadly, where there is a 'front', there is no trust. Without trust there can be no relationship. What is life without relationships? Empty. Where are true relationships born? In the heart. Love from the center of who you are; don't fake it. Romans 12:9–10 (MSG).

"I must curb my rhetoric."

Jannie smiled. She could see the passion Mr. Sherman had for this subject of the heart. It made her even more convinced she should glean everything she could from this man.

"Let's see. Where were we?" Mr. Sherman paused for a few moments while he looked at the first several pages of his notebook.

"In my opinion, the subject of the heart is misunderstood," stated Mr. Sherman without looking up from his notebook. "I believe it comes from the fact we can't see it. Oh, we talk about it all the time, but do we really know what it is?

"We know beliefs reside in the heart (Romans 10:10). For with the heart man believes. The beliefs that are stored in the heart are evidenced by what comes out of our mouths. Out of the abundance of the heart, the mouth speaks (Luke 6:45).

"The other day we talked about forgiveness being the beginning of healing for the heart. The outcome of forgiveness is peace for the person who forgives. When we do not forgive, we run the risk of hardening our hearts and becoming bitter.

"The Bible talks about having a root of bitterness in the New Testament," Jannie commented.

"Yes, the root of bitterness. How do you interpret that? Well, I don't believe the way it is worded in English correctly expresses what it was meant to convey in the original language. When it is quoted in Hebrews 12:15, Paul mentions the root of bitterness springing up. It is often assumed that bitterness is the root. But you can see bitterness in people, right? I believe that is actually the fruit. Look, for instance, at the wording of 1 Timothy 6:10, which states the 'love of money is the root of all evil'. When we leave out the word 'all', there remains the 'root of evil'. And what is the root of evil? The love of money. Therefore, it is the 'love' that is the root and the 'evil' is the fruit. So what is root of bitterness? Deuteronomy 29:18 talks about 'a root BEARING poisonous and bitter fruit'. If the bitterness is the fruit, what is the root? The answer seems to be in the next verse 'walking in stubborness of heart'. I believe the hardened heart produces bitterness.

"So how do we go about our lives and not harden our hearts after we suffer traumatic experiences?" Jannie asked.

"Well, I wrote down a quote from Dr. Jim Richards of Impact Ministries. He says, 'The experiences we have in life literally abide in us'. As a matter of fact, the Book of Jeremiah 17:9 states in the King James Version, 'The heart is deceitful above all things and desperately wicked'. Well the word *deceitful* is literally the word *footprints*. It's saying that our heart has footprints, and it is very chaotic. These footprints, we now understand, are the frequencies or the cellular memories that are recorded in the cells of our body.

"Trauma and abuse imprint on the heart. It is not the actual circumstance that causes the hurt but the negative thoughts, emotions and fear created by the event. The impact of these emotional wounds, now resident in the heart, will influence all future decisions until they are healed and ultimately removed. Again, I believe this goes back to forgiving. We can't change the past, but we must do everything in our power to remove ourselves from traumatic situations. And then for our own sakes, we must forgive. Forgiving others empowers us to get our lives back. I believe it is the beginning to changing the footprints that are stored in the heart. Forgiveness is about us getting healed, not about what someone did to us.

"Again, I don't think we should try to do this on our own. If you are in a bad situation, cry out for help. If you don't find it immediately, try someone else. Someone is always willing to help. There is no shame in seeking out counselling."

Jannie looked up from her laptop. She had been frantically typing, trying to keep up with Mr. Sherman's thought train.

"Ahem," Ms. Brookes cleared her throat to attract Mr. Sherman's attention.

"Oh," I didn't hear you come in."

"I wanted to let you know I will be going to the bank and running a few other errands. I will be back within the hour," announced Ms. Brookes.

"Oh, no problem." Mr. Sherman smiled. Jannie studied the interaction between employer and employee. She thought she almost detected a hint of a smile on Ms. Brookes' face, but she couldn't be sure. Ms. Brookes left the room as quickly as she had entered it.

Jannie looked at Mr. Sherman inquisitively. Her expression was begging to know more about Ms. Brookes and who she was behind her straight-laced exterior. Jannie didn't dare say what she was thinking. If Mr. Sherman read her facial expression, he did not let on. Maybe he hadn't figured her out yet, either. On the other hand, maybe he had.

Trauma and abuse imprint on the heart. It is not the actual circumstance that causes the hurt but the negative thoughts, emotions and fear created by the event.

Mr. Sherman looked intently through his huge leather-bound book, flipping pages and then pausing.

"When we look at why people do what they do, it comes down to motives. Where does motivation come from? It comes from the heart, of course. Sometimes, actions appear to say one thing about a person, but if you dig a bit deeper, the motivation actually says the opposite."

"Like the guy in Proverbs 23:7, eat and drink he says, but his heart is not with you? asked Jannie.

"Yes, but more specifically, it is about doing something on the outside and for a completely different reason."

"I know. There's another example of Performance-based relationships!" exclaimed Jannie.

"That is an interesting observation."

"It's like you said; persons' actions look like they are doing something nice for you, but the real intent is to gain favor with you," explained Jannie. Getting points, as my brother Ed called it. But like my dad said, there is no points system—either with women or with God."

"I agree," said Mr. Sherman. "I knew a gentleman who was a deacon in a church for more than 30 years. He was the first to show up whenever there was a service. He had the key to the church and would arrive ahead of everyone else. He would do all the behind-the-scenes work like preparing for communion. The trouble is, even though he was physically present in church, he never made a heart connection with God. When he finally did, he was so amazed that he had wasted all those years performing tasks while his heart lay dormant. I cannot judge why this fellow would have done all these acts of service for years. Perhaps he was trying to gain favour with God. Perhaps he thought that was the way to get into heaven. The Bible teaches the opposite, though. According to what Apostle Paul wrote in Ephesians 2, our salvation is a gift from God and not obtained by works, so no one can boast.

According to what Apostle Paul wrote in Ephesians 2, our salvation is a gift from God and not obtained by works, so no one can boast.

"So, just as actions can come from a different motivation than is initially perceived, trying to change behaviour without changing motivation is futile. Simply telling a person what behaviour is expected of them in order to get them to change their actions might work in the short term, but it often doesn't last. They may do so at the beginning, but their heart is not in it. See, when we try to change the circumstances from the outside instead of initiating change from the inside, we end up with behaviour modification only. It seems to me, we cannot truly change behaviour until we change the motivation.

"I think we get too caught up in criticizing what we see with our eyes and neglect to look into the influencing factors. I am glad God is not like that. We know the story of King David in the Bible. God called him a man after His own heart (Acts 13:22). Yet one of the most famous stories of David is of him committing adultery and then murder to cover it up. How could God even look at him after he had messed up so badly? I think the answer is in 1 Samuel 16:7: 'for God sees not as man sees, for man looks at the outward appearance, but the LORD looks at the heart' NASB.

"God is always seeking people after His own heart. II Chronicles 16:9 says, 'For the eyes of the Lord run to and fro throughout the whole earth, to show Himself strong on behalf of those whose heart is perfect or blameless toward Him or loyal to Him'.

"God is seeking someone in whose life He can exhibit His power. What are the criteria? A loyal heart and a blameless heart. The King James Version calls it 'a perfect heart'. Why does it not say He wants perfect actions or a perfect attitude? Because it is what resides in the heart that steers the life of a man. In chapter 3 of the Book of James, it says 'the tongue is the rudder of the whole body, steering it through life'. It does not take a rocket scientist to figure out that the ball of flesh that we label the tongue is not capable of initiating any speech. The activity of speech is triggered by the brain. But as we know from Matthew 12:34, 'the words come from what is the heart in abundance'.

"But let us not stop there. Look at the end of II Chronicles 16:9: 'In this you have done foolishly; therefore from now on you shall have wars'. The King of Judah, whom this passage was written to, chose not to rely on the Lord in fighting his battles. Therefore, he reaped the consequences and the results were the loss of battle.

"It's interesting to see that we haven't learned much since then. The prophet sent to the King on behalf of the Lord was basically saying, 'God knows what's going on, He can guide you but you have to be in tune with Him'. Since God communicates to man through his spirit—another name for heart—when our heart is tuned toward Him, He can direct our steps to victory. But like many of us would, the king took offence, threw the prophet in prison, and died a short time later.

"God is constantly on the look out for those who will yield their hearts to Him. He is all about the heart!"

Mr. Sherman sat back in his chair and exhaled a relaxed breath. He folded his hands across his book with his elbows resting on each of the raised chair arms.

Jannie took it as a sign they were done for the afternoon and began to gather her things. "You don't have to see me out. Just stay here and relax."

"I think I will, Jannie. As usual, it has been a pleasure.

Jannie decended the stairs to the front walk when she heard a familiar voice.

"Care for a ride?" Derek called out to her. "Your mom said you were taking the bus today."

"Where did you get this car?" Jannie held her mouth open in a mock state of shock.

"It belongs to my friend Jordan. He asked me to housesit while he is away this weekend, and he tossed me the key as he was going out the door. He told me that I should enjoy it before it has to be put away for the season. Come on, jump in."

Jannie slid onto the moulded leather bucket seat next to Derek. A console with a gearshift divided them. The top had been retracted and tucked neatly under a buttoned leather cover just above the back seat. Jannie looked around at the 360-degree view.

"Here, you will probably need these." Derek handed her a pair of sunglasses that had no particular style to them. "You might want to tie your hair back as well." His eyes surveyed her as if taking stock of every detail.

Without warning, Derek revved the motor and sped down the narrow road to the highway. He weaved the red convertible in and out of traffic on the edge of breaking the law without actually going over the speed limit. Jannie scrunched up her face as to block the oncoming force of the wind. At times, her hair blew straight back, perpendicular to its normal position. It was almost too cold to be riding with the top down. This would infinitely be the last ride of the season.

God knows what's going on, He can guide you but you have to be in tune with Him.

Derek slowed for a traffic light, slid the transmission into neutral and revved the engine again. He gazed over at her and grinned. His expression said it all—the schoolboy on the first day with his new toy. It didn't seem to matter to him that it wasn't his car. Nobody knew. Jannie was too shy to look in either direction in case people were staring.

"You look good behind the wheel," was her only comment, and they sped off again making it too noisy to talk.

Dad was getting out of his car when they pulled into the driveway.

"My goodness," exclaimed Dad. "I thought for a minute it was Ed pulling one of his usual stunts. You know, arriving in a whirlwind, unannounced."

"I guess Ed is wearing off on Derek," said Jannie as she tried to run her fingers through her tangled hair. No use. It was beyond fixing without the help of a stiff brush. She grabbed her handbag and headed up the front walk.

"What's a college kid like you doing in a car like that anyway?" Dad asked.

"Just getting used to what it will be like when I have a successful career like you," Derek jested. Dad laughed a hearty laugh.

"Nice car!" Mom called from the porch. "Are you staying for dinner?"

"I suppose I could," Derek said hesitantly.

Jannie shot him a sideways glance. "You do know that means you will have to help prepare it."

"I can do all things." he drawled.

CHAPTER 10

JANNIE SAT AT THE EDGE OF THE SOFA WITH HER laptop open on the coffee table in front of her. The cat wove its way silently through her legs. It wound back and forth about three times before it made its way over to the glass patio doors. There, it made itself into a complete ball and watched the drama of the outside world unfold under its attentive eye. Jannie looked over at it and wondered what it was thinking. Sometimes, life might be a lot less complicated if she were a cat. But then it would not be as exhilarating. She picked up her coffee cup to reveal a coaster with a quote from Ralph Waldo Emerson. She replaced her coffee onto the coaster. Upside down at the other end of the coffee table was a well-worn book—a novel from what she could guess. She reached over and flipped it up so she could read the title. No, not a novel. As Jannie's mind continued to subconsciously take in insignificant thoughts, she could feel something. She needed to stop and close her eyes and listen intently to her heart. It was saying something. Something big.

Jannie began to recall incidents that stuck out in her mind about heart issues. She called to mind the conversation she overheard in the college library while she was studying for exams. Two men were discussing relationships when one made the comment, "I left my girlfriend a long time ago; she just doesn't know it yet."

What was he saying? He had disconnected from her emotionally. Essentially, he had withdrawn his heart. From what she could interpret, the relationship was doomed to failure after that.

She remembered her parents sitting for hours with her mother's sister several years ago when her marriage had ended because of infidelity. Jannie had not understood the many complicated aspects of relationships at the time but part of the conversations stuck out in her mind. "Infidelity begins in the heart," she had overheard. "If a partner is unwilling or unable to connect intimately on a heart level, the other will begin to seek intimacy elsewhere. When a couple comes together, there must be intimacy of heart before there can be physical intimacy or else it is just sex."

He had disconnected from her emotionally. Essentially, he had withdrawn his heart. From what she could interpret, the relationship was doomed to failure after that.

Many late nights had been spent in their living room, helping her aunt work through painful issues. She recalled another couple that had been brought in to help with counselling. One of them had cautioned, "Before making a judgement on someone who 'fooled around' on his spouse, consider there are always two different people in the relationship, and we are only observing from the outside and seeing the result of what may have taken place. The infidelity shows up in one partner and immediately we see them as the cheater or sinner. However, what went on prior to the act of infidelity that created an atmosphere for wanting to change partners? A colleague of mine worded it like this: 'If you have steak at home, why would you go out for hamburger?' Translation: if your partner is meeting your needs to the point that you hold your relationship in high esteem, there is little or no chance that when conflicts arise, neither partner would ever consider going anywhere else. If, however, you have a neglectful or non-understanding partner, or if your partner is constantly trying to correct you, control you or change you to fit the mould they have in mind for you, something inside is going to snap. That, I believe, is when infidelity is born. It is basically a result or symptom of a greater need that is not being met. We all have an inherent need to be loved and valued. If that is constantly withheld or denied, we are driven elsewhere. I'm not saying that is the correct response. I am just identifying the underlying cause. When I hear of a relationship breakup because one of the partners went to someone else, my first thought is what went on in the relationship to cause the straying partner to want to leave?"

Jannie took another sip of coffee. Yuck, it was cold. She reclined on the couch and stared at the ceiling. Her mind drifted back to a time when Ed had pursued a girl from Jannie's class in high school. He had tried desperately to get her to go out with him but she refused. When he finally convinced Jannie to intervene on his behalf, the girl had simply said, "I can't. I gave my heart to someone else." The statement had more impact on Jannie now than it did at the time of hearing it. Spending time with Mr. Sherman had caused her to begin seeing life through different eyes. She was more analytical. She began looking for things behind the scenes rather than taking everything she saw for face value.

Sadness washed over her as she remembered when, a few years ago, a well-known comedian had committed suicide. It had shocked the world. Many advocate groups began pushing for more funding to be funnelled into mental health organisations. Like them, she wished the comedian had reached out to get help before it was too late. Now, looking back, she wondered if it was a mental health issue. Maybe that was not the correct diagnosis. Could it be he had unresolved hurts in his heart that caused him so much pain that he couldn't go on living? Not that labelling an issue as mental, spiritual or emotional should make any difference in the long run. Or did it? What if wrong labelling led to misdiagnosis? It would be very dangerous if misdiagnosis turned into wrong treatment. That brought her to another thought. Could misdiagnosis of issues actually be worse for people than no diagnosis at all? Hmmm, the jury was still out on that one.

Jannie closed her laptop and slid it into its protective case. It was decision-making time. From Proverbs 20:5, she knew "The intentions of a person's heart are deep waters but a discerning person reveals them." Mr. Sherman would be key in helping direct her on the right path.

When she arrived at Mr. Sherman's that afternoon, he was there to greet her at the door. The elation that permeated his whole being could not be hidden.

"I have fabulous news, Jannie. My wife is being released from the care facility. She's coming home!"

"Oh, my!" Jannie didn't know whether to laugh or cry or do both simultaneously. Instead she spontaneously grabbed Mr. Sherman's hands and pulled him into an embrace. "I am soooooooo happy for you! When does she arrive?"

"Well, there are a few details to work through first. The liaisons are securing care workers who will live in during the first phase. There is also a bit of upgrading to the home. Nothing major. A few support bars will be installed, but they assured me she would be here no later than the end of the week."

"Ahhh," Jannie squealed. "It is your dream come true!"

"Yes, it is all coming together as I had hoped." His smile was contagious. "The workers at the care facility cautioned me not to get my hopes up. But I knew better. Let me tell you what I know about hope." They made their way to the library where Mr. Sherman was already prepared with his notebook. He leafed through a few tabs on the side of the pages until he found one labeled 'hope'. "Here it is. Write this down. You never know when you will need it."

"If you have no hope, there is nothing with which to anchor your faith. Faith is the substance of things hoped for according to Hebrews 11:1. You won't receive the things you need or want from God without faith—without faith it is is impossible to please him (Hebrews 11:6), but you can't use your faith if you have no hope. Get your hopes up! Get your hope activated. Hope deferred makes the heart sick (Proverbs 13:12). Many people are sick in their heart because they have lost hope. I believe there is no such thing as false hope, only false definitions of hope. And hope does not disappoint us (Romans 5:5). Hope that is seen is not hope (Romans 8:24). In 1 Peter 1:3, He has given us a living hope through Jesus.

"Jannie, do not reduce your dreams to fit what you see in the natural. Get your hopes up and start dreaming your way out of your current situation."

Many people are sick in their heart because they have lost hope. I believe there is no such thing as false hope, only false definitions of hope.

By now Jannie had pulled out her laptop and recorded what Mr. Sherman had spoken. She found it was faster to type than to take notes on paper. "So when you say the word hope, it is not synonymous with the word *wish*, correct?"

"Ah, you learn quickly, my girl. Hope activated becomes a knowing that what you desire will come to pass."

"Speaking of desires," Jannie began.

"Wait a moment," he interrupted. "Before you make that final decision, let me read you something from Pastor Rick Renner. 'The greatest tragedy you could ever experience is to let go of your God-given dream and allow the fire in your heart to go out. To do that is the equivalent of letting go of your special individuality, your divine call, and your God-given giftings'."

> The greatest tragedy you could ever experience is to let go of your God-given dream and allow the fire in your heart to go out.

Just then, in a split second, unannounced, the revelation hit her. It was as if it had been downloaded into her and became visible on an imaginary screen before her eyes. It was all clear. She stared at Mr. Sherman.

"I think—," she halted in mid thought, fixating on his expression. His face said it all.

He knew! He had known all along. He had been waiting the whole time for her to come to the realization on her own. Mr. Sherman had spent years studying, documenting and cataloging information about the heart, knowing it had to be shared. He had wanted it published, but it was not for him to write. He had purposely fed her this knowledge because he could see the bigger picture.

As if on cue, the large grandfather clock outside the room chimed out the hour.

Without another word, the two rose from their seats and began to make their way to the front door. Derek would be here soon to pick up Jannie. She and Mr. Sherman waited for him in the foyer.

This would be the last formal session between her and the elder gentleman. Both of them would wake up tomorrow and start their lives on different paths. He would welcome his wife home—an event he had awaited for a long time. Although things were changing, it was not a real goodbye. Jannie vowed to herself to visit the Shermans every chance she got.

"If I may give you one last parting piece of advice, Jannie."

"Sure, what is it?"

"Stay away from both causing offence and taking offence. It's been said that people who are hurting will hurt other people. Similarly, I believe offended people offend other people. In other words, those who offend are the ones who themselves live a life of habitual offence. James 3:2 says, 'If any man offend not in word, the same is a perfect man'. Keep your life free from offence. It is the biggest killer of relationships." Jannie looked at him inquisitively.

"When a person takes offence at another's words or actions, it damages their relationship. Maybe the offender was having a bad day or maybe his comment was misinterpreted. Maybe the offended person is too sensitive or maybe one doesn't agree with the other's opinion or view of the world. Regardless of the situation, we have opportunities to be offended every day. The less we take those opportunities, the better off we are."

"That's excellent. I should write that down."

"No, Jannie, you should live by it." There was a long pause.

"Derek should be here any minute," she said, changing the subject. She had decided she would wait until they were all together before she made her big announcement.

"I see you two have been spending a lot of time together lately."

"Yes," Jannie blushed. "He's a very good friend."

"I would hazard a guess he is wanting to be more than just your friend." There was a slight lilt in his voice. Jannie stood motionless. Speechless, she turned abruptly. Mr. Sherman's eyes were soft and he looked as if his whole being was smiling. It was as if he had read a part of her soul that she was not even aware was there. He had boldly declared what she had not dared to think.

Mr. Sherman spoke softly, "I suggest that if he asks you an important question, you consider saying yes." Tears instantly welled up in her eyes. To her surprise, she began to laugh. Mr. Sherman put his arm around her and squeezed her shoulder, supporting the weight of both of them on his cane.

"He is a very fine young man, Jannie. Forget all the advice about considering what he looks like and what personality traits he has. More important than personality is character. There is a difference. Although personality is desirable in a casual social setting, character is what you need to look at deeply when choosing a mate. If he has your best interest at heart, everything else will work itself out."

"Thank you," she breathed. She slid her hand inside her pocket and produced a tissue to dab at the moisture in her eyes. Mr. Sherman grinned. Behind her, she heard footsteps approaching. Derek, obviously able to see them standing there, was letting himself in the door.

He straightened his large solid frame and looked wide-eyed at the pair. "So, don't keep me in suspense," he said eagerly. "What have you decided?"

Jannie looked down at her shoes trying to draw attention away from her. She inhaled a deep breath.

"I have decided to return to college this upcoming semester," meeting his gaze with a smile.

"And—," coaxed Derek, having sensed there was more.

"And—," she started hesitantly. Derek circled his hands in a gesture that was his way of saying, 'come on, out with it'.

"I will spend the next six months writing a thesis. I already have many of the notes. I am calling it, "It's All About the Heart."

"Interesting."

Mr. Sherman clasped his hands and nodded his approval.

Derek raised his eyebrows. "I like it, I think." Jannie's sigh relieved a lot of the tension she held until this moment.

Although personality is desirable in a casual social setting, character is what you need to look at deeply when choosing a mate.

Derek cupped Jannie's elbow with his hand to lead her to the door. But she turned and leaped toward Mr. Sherman for one last hug.

"Thank you sooooooo much for everything," she said. "This has been an amazing journey."

"This is not goodbye, though." We still have many more tea times to enjoy. And this time, Isabella will be able to join us. Oh, she is going to love it!"

Derek opened the door and gently steered Jannie out onto the step outside. As they walked toward the car, she stopped and turned to see Mr. Sherman standing at the door waving. She waved back and slid into the front seat of Derek's late model sedan. It wasn't nearly the calibre of car he had driven the last time he picked her up. She did not mind, though. This one was comfortable and warm.

As they drove away, Derek silently grasped her hand in his, his gaze fixed on the road ahead. Jannie did not look at him but stared straight in front of her. His grip was gentle but strong. A grip that indicated to Jannie he did not want to let go. She didn't want him to either.

About the Author

 Lenore Schur was born and raised in small-town Saskatchewan on the Canadian Prairies. She began writing her first novel at age 11 in longhand on foolscap paper, but she shelved her manuscript when cramps in her hand set in after 14 handwritten pages. But her love of writing was born, and it would manifest in one form or another throughout the rest of her life. Her first magazine article was published in 1989, and she went on to work as a staff writer for a magazine publisher. As a freelance writer, she later wrote magazine articles and advertising copy for tourism publications. *It's All About the Heart* is her first novel.

Resources

For additional information on heart matters, please visit the following online resources:

The Hurt Pocket **Video Series by Pastor Jimmy Evans**
https://www.rightnow.org/Content/Series/482

Forgiveness from the Heart **Audio Series by Craig Hill**
https://www.familyfoundations.com/product/forgiveness-from-the-heart-cds/

20/20 Gods Vision for My Life **CDs by Pastor Robert Morris**
http://gatewaypeople.lightspeedwebstore.com/20-20-gods-vision-for-my-life-cds-210000002027/dp/1939

Essential Heart Physics **Series by Dr. James B. Richards**
http://www.impactministries.com/?s=essential+heart+physics